Bes

MW01137747

"The emotions are so raw and powerful, amazing in a such a short piece. You could practically taste the emotions rolling off of the characters: the fear, the anger, the rage, the grief, and even the love."
~ *Kim Deister, The Caffeinated Diva Reviews.*

"Frantic moments of suppressed terror will grip you when you read this tale of desperation and lost control. Truly gripping!"
~ *Lacey Weatherford, Author Of Witches and Warlocks series.*

"Heartwarming characters and a sexy hero come together to make a wonderful read in Belinda Boring's CHERISHED."
~ *The Romance Reviews.*

"Call the folks over at Merriam Webster and let them know of an immediate change: the word "romance" should now include a cover picture of Mystic Wolves. Seriously, I haven't read such a truly romantic story in a long time."
~ *Laurie, Reader Girls.*

"Just when I thought everything was fine and dandy and happily ever after then boom, she does it again! Another cliffhanger! One that just nearly knocked me off my chair! Now I must have to wait to see what happens. Write faster please I have to know!"
~ *Donna, Book Lover's Hideaway.*

"This was awesome! It had a little bit of everything. There was death, happiness, love, kidnapping and a home wrecker. I laughed, I cried, and I swooned. How could you not love it?"
~ *Kacey Stewart.*

THE *Mystic* WOLVES

Mystic Wolves Series Book One

Belinda Boring

Moonstruck Media
ARIZONA

Mystic Wolves
Copyright © 2012 Belinda Boring

ALL RIGHTS RESERVED
ISBN-13: **978-1469926902**
ISBN-10: **1469926903**

Published by

Moonstruck Media
Arizona

Dedication

To my husband, Mark

What man sits for hours, watching his favorite TV
show on mute so his wife can write?
You. For that (and much more), you have my heart
and soul forever. Thank you for believing in me. I love
you.

To a greatly missed confidante, Craig

Thank you for encouraging me to write, even when
I was adamant that I had nothing to say. It's okay for
you to say, "I told you so." I deserve it. *grins*

Acknowledgments

When I think about the process of writing the Mystic Wolves, I realize there were so many people who joined me for this journey, whose influence can be found anywhere from helping to develop it, to the story itself.

As always, I am forever grateful to my best friend, Lacey. She has been a guiding force these last few months, and I honestly don't know what I'd do without her. She's one of my greatest cheerleaders and defenders, someone who has always believed in me and the stories I want to share. Whether it was going for drives to discuss the storyline or giggling over editing, I'm just so grateful for all she's done.

There is a group of people, friends who quickly became family, that I know have played an amazing role in not just my life, but also my writing. They are all incredible writers, sharing their talents freely and always there with a smile and heart whenever I needed it. I'm not quite sure they realize just how much they've inspired me, helping me find the confidence I was lacking. They are an important part of my day, and I'm honored to know them.

I would really love to thank those I chat with on Facebook. Don't let anybody fool you or try to say that social media is a waste of time. I have met so many incredible people, shared laughter and tears with them, and without a doubt, have been blessed by the way each of you have touched my life. Thank you for your acceptance and support. Thank you for putting up with my random status comments. But most of all, thank you for letting me swoon with you!

And finally, my deepest love to my husband, Mark. Whether it was listening to me work through the plot, making sure I had everything I needed to stay up all night, sending lunchtime texts just to see how I was doing, or running me a bath when I was exhausted and needed to think—he was there when I needed him most. You truly do remind me of Mason!

Bels

Chapter One

"Quit your posturing, Daniel, and hike the ball!"

I couldn't help but laugh at the serious tone coming from Mason as he growled at his best friend. Looking around at the others on the make shift field, I turned to Jasmine and rolled my eyes.

"What is it with men and football? Don't they know it's just a game?" I brushed a strand of hair away from my eyes as I looked over to see the play. Daniel finally sent the ball to the quarterback, and after that it was just a blur.

Mason quickly faked, running through his team as they opened up a path for him. He twisted out of the grasp of some of the opposing players, but Jonas was no match for him. I winced at the sound of bodies hitting at full force, and for the hundredth time that afternoon, wondered why I was watching.

The sun was hot, beating down on the Pack, as we enjoyed a peaceful Sunday afternoon together. Mason had called everyone in for a game and food—the men getting their macho groove on first, and then once their blood thirstiness was appeased, they'd let the women play too.

"Don't let them hear you say that, Darcy. Last time you did, you almost started a war, and that was just with my brother." Jasmine glanced over at Mason with a soft smile. I reached over to give her a quick hug. By becoming the future mate of the Mystic Wolves Alpha, not only did I gain someone to love forever, but I was also blessed with a best friend, sister, and confidante. Or, depending on what mischief we got up to, a partner in crime and fellow conspirator. Our favorite targets—Mason and Daniel.

"He talked to me like I was stupid. How was I to know there was actual strategy to the game? As far as I knew, it was just a bunch of guys standing around, slapping butts, and taking a million breaks in between passing the ball around." I scoffed.

"Well, you didn't help your case by calling them wusses. I'm pretty sure you offended their sense of masculine pride. I swear Daniel practically beat his chest at you." She covered her mouth to hide her giggle, her gaze darting over to the object of her crush. "I'll admit he did look adorable doing it."

"Yeah, me Daniel ... you woman who should be in kitchen cooking." I thumped myself, doing my best to represent a caveman. "And he's mild compared to Mr. Alpha-Super-Protective over there." I pointed toward Mason, feeling a flush of desire at the way his t-shirt clung tightly to his torso.

"So what does that say about us? You're desperately in love with my brother, and I can't quite shake the way Daniel makes me giddy when he looks at me."

"It makes us women who know what we want, even if it means we're crazy about a bunch of dorks." The sound of shouting brought our attention to the field, and I groaned loudly, the sight before us a complete mess.

It was a free for all—bodies piled by the sideline, and I couldn't quite tell who was on the bottom. Whoever it was I felt for them because all that weight ... it had to hurt.

Mason rose to his feet, and began digging through the rubble. Grabbing shirts randomly, he soon everyone pulled off the poor fool at the base of the heap. Jonas was slow to stand, looking a little drunk as he swayed back and forth. With a few hearty back slaps from his team, he shook his head as if to clear something and broke out into a wide smile.

"Neanderthals, I swear one day they're going to kill themselves." I snorted loudly, not caring who heard. Of course Mason did, and he winked at me. I poked my tongue at him and his voice echoed in my mind.

Tease.

I blew him a kiss and looked on in horror as I saw Eric come barreling toward him. The impact of the hit sent Mason soaring through the air, much to the entertainment of the team.

"Darcy, whatever you're doing, knock it off! We need Mason to focus, and he can't do that if he's making goofy eyes at you." Daniel yelled out, and was joined with the agreement of the others. Shrugging my shoulders slightly, I offered a small apology and breathed a sigh of relief when I saw Mason standing. As if nothing had happened, he got back into formation, waiting for the ball.

A quick snap and pass to Daniel saw him leaping over a tackle, before running to the end for a touchdown. Cheers rose in the air, and I whistled loudly as I watched Daniel and Wade chest bump.

"Yay! You got another goal! I'm so proud of you guys!" I cupped my hands around my mouth, and hollered loudly. I was rewarded with a chorus of corrections.

"You do know it's called a touchdown, right? This isn't soccer," Jasmine whispered.

"Of course, but it's worth having them remind me when I forget. I seriously think Mason risks losing his eyeballs if they rolled any farther back into his head."

"You're so bad. I love it!" Jasmine knocked

shoulders with me, and I reached over to grab hold of her hand.

"What else is there to do but torment the ones we love, huh? Oh, it's your turn too by the way." Looking around, I could see her thinking.

"Hmmm, what haven't we used yet today?" She took in a deep breath, and then let out an almighty cry. "Come on, slackers. You call this a game? Shoot and score already!"

Mason raised his hand to his mouth, releasing a shrill whistle and signaled for a time out.

"You're in for it now. Wonder how long it'll take for him to start lecturing us?" I whispered quietly, watching the teams separate into their own huddles. Mason shared a few short commands before he started jogging over to where we were sitting.

"Hey babe, looking good out there. Is it almost time for us to join in? Jasmine and I have been practicing since the last time." I flashed an innocent look, trying to hide the wicked grin I could feel under the surface. He gave me a look that melted my insides before pointing his finger at the both of us.

"What have I told you two about haggling from the sidelines?" he questioned sternly.

"Not to do it because it's distracting," I began.

"Because we sound silly yelling out nonsense," Jasmine finished.

We answered him as though he was a teacher, repeating back his instructions in singsong voices. There was a brief pause before we broke into laughter, and it only became worse as he scowled.

"Come on, it's funny. Admit it, you love every moment of it, and it's the highlight of the game." I reached to touch him, but the feel of his sweaty shirt made pull back my hand. He caught the action, and a mischievous twinkle lit up his eyes.

"You know me so well, Darcy." He closed the distance between us, and I realized what he was up to.

"Oh no you don't, Mason O'Connor. You take that sweaty body of yours back over to your team mates and do some ... I don't know ... male bonding or something." With my arms outstretched to ward of his attempts to hold me, I wasn't strong enough to keep him away.

Iron bands enclosed me, dragging me from my seat and into his embrace. I struggled slightly, trying to appear as though I was escaping, but I was exactly where I wanted to be—in the arms of the man I loved.

He leaned in. I couldn't stop myself from reaching out and pulling his face to mine. His heady mixture of man, wolf, and sunshine was intoxicating—alluring. I forgot the world around me as I brushed my mouth against his.

He hadn't shaved, soft stubble grazing against my skin, and it caused goose bumps to rise as it created friction. Parting my lips, I felt his tongue slip in and begin to tangle against mine. I went into sensory overload. Everything about this man aroused me, and I melted willingly into his tight embrace. I couldn't get close enough.

The game was forgotten—all that existed was him and me. His hand reached into my hair, holding my head in place, and I groaned into his mouth as he deepened our kiss. If this was the kind of punishment I would receive for taunting him, I was determined to up the ante. I whimpered with disappointment when he slowly broke away, my flesh tingling everywhere he'd touched. He rendered me senseless, and I couldn't help the goofy grin that covered my face.

Lifting my fingers to trace my lips once more, hunger burning deep, I stumbled backward and was brought out of my daze by Jasmine's giggle.

"Was that really necessary, Brother?" she questioned, slapping him hard against his shoulder. "How are we supposed to come in and wow you all with our football skills, if you've addled her brain? Look at her, she can barely focus."

"I think she looks sexy as hell."

My heart began racing faster, Mason stepping forward to take me back into his arms. Like a magnet that can't fight against its attraction, I moved toward him, only to meet with Jasmine's arm.

"Leave her be. Go back and prepare to get your butts handed to you. I need to undo the damage." She shooed him away with a flick of her wrist, and tugged on my arm.

"Has anyone told you how adorable you are when you attempt to trash talk?"

I began to chuckle at the stern look on Jasmine's face.

"Well, at least she's snapping out of it. Come on, Darcy. We've work to do."

Shrugging my shoulders in a sign of helpless submission, I allowed myself to be pulled toward the house. "Did you really need to interrupt?" I complained, the taste of the kiss still in my mouth. "You couldn't have let me enjoy him just a little longer? He is my mate."

She rolled her eyes, and snorted. "Future mate—and you both have plenty of time for all the lovey-dovey stuff. Right now, we have a game to win, so pull yourself together and help me."

Opening the door to her bedroom, my thoughts finally settled back on the task at hand. "Okay, what do you have planned?"

Digging around in the small bag on her dresser, Jasmine held up an eyeliner pencil, a wide grin spread across her face. "Just a little fun."

And she got down to business.

Chapter Two

As I crouched down into a stance, I snarled menacingly at the player facing me. I tried to channel mean, vicious thoughts, and a sense of I-will-dominate-you, but all it managed to do was make me giggle.

"You call that intimidating? That scowl wouldn't even scare a kitten, and what is that under your eyes?" Daniel replied, trying not to look at me. Every time he did, I pulled a face—this time sticking my tongue out to the side and scrunching my nose. I fought the urge to wipe at the black smudges. I'd seen players on T.V. do the same, and it was all part of my plan to distract and conquer.

"It's war paint. Like it?" I beamed back at him widely.

He shook his head, clearly not impressed. "You look silly. Both you and Jasmine."

I looked to where she was standing, focusing on her own target, and whistled for her attention. She glanced over, and I started signaling my intentions for Daniel, ending with a fierce fist bash against my palm. Jasmine laughed out loud, giving me two thumbs up. This caused Daniel to groan, and I rolled my eyes.

"It's okay to admit it—I have you quaking in fear. I promise I won't tell your pack brothers." I winked, hearing the sound of the next call being announced by Mason. Playing defense, I had to make sure I stopped Daniel from opening up a space for his Alpha to run through. I might be small, but if he thought my lack of size wasn't something to worry about, he was in for a rude shock. I hadn't been lying about practicing, and although Devlin didn't play football often, he still knew a few tricks.

The ball snapped, Mason trying another fake, and Daniel erupted into movement. Determined to squash him, I launched my own body, using my shoulder to connect with his lower half and was rewarded with an oomph. Caught off guard by the power behind my charge, Daniel went flying, and I couldn't help the smug look of satisfaction as I stood over him.

"Scared now?" I dusted my hands off as I peered down into his face. His initial reaction was one of disbelief, but it was soon replaced with one of pride.

"Damn, girl. Where did you learn to hit like that?" He reached his hand out for assistance, and I pulled him up, centering my balance to keep myself from falling on top of him.

"I can have my secrets." I kept my answer brief, letting him wonder all he wanted. I lifted my two fingers to my eyes, signaling I was watching him. "Think I can do that again?" I knew I was messing with fire when I saw the question light something in his gaze, but I didn't care. I loved playing with the pack.

"Prepare yourself then, and don't go complaining to the Alpha when you break a nail." He grinned wickedly, knowing his piggish comment would raise my ire.

"You are such a jerk sometimes, Daniel. Did I ever tell you that?" I watched him listen for the next play, and he got ready. His attention never left my face, and he mouthed the words you are mine.

Even though I could see him coming, nothing prepared me for the smoothness of motion as the ball hiked back, and he raced forward to stop me. It was move or be crushed by a hulking werewolf, and a squeal erupted from me. I scrambled, barely able to twist from his outstretched grasp, and seeing I was in the clear, I focused on Mason. He was looking for an opening—a receiver to throw the ball to, and he swung his arm back to aim.

"Penalty!" I screamed.

The game came to a grinding halt, and everyone turned to look at me. Mason tilted his head, looking to see what had gone wrong, confusion blazing on his face. I didn't blame him as I was clearly standing alone, the closest player to me being Eric, and he wasn't within arm's reach.

"Why'd you call a foul, Darcy? What did you see?" Jonas wandered over, ready to help.

"I want to call an illegal face mask against the quarterback." I tried to look as serious as possible, my hands resting on my hips. "That's a fifty yard penalty, right? Move them back."

"Darcy?" Eric shouted out. "You're not even wearing a helmet!"

The pack erupted into laughter, and Mason looked like he didn't know whether he wanted to chuckle or throttle me. He knew exactly what I'd done and why—if the throw had connected, they would've scored a touchdown.

"Oh, my bad." I shrugged my shoulders, trying to appear sheepish. "I guess we can keep going then." I returned back to my position, and hunkered down.

"I'm calling a penalty then." Mason broke away from his team members, heading straight for me. "Against Darcy ... for wrongful interference." The twinkle in his eye gave him away. He felt like being playful too.

"I didn't interfere. It was an honest mistake, how was I to know?" I answered, twirling my finger around in my ponytail. "You wouldn't hold that against me, would you?" I bat my eyelashes, causing his step to falter slightly. "Besides, how do I know there's even a call like that? You could be making it up."

"I'm the Alpha, what I say is law. I declare you interfered in my play and need to be punished."

Pack members stepped away, and gathered closely so they could get a clear view of what would happen next. Mason and I were an affectionate couple, but our small disputes were also legendary. This could go either way, and Daniel let out a howl of encouragement in the background.

"You teach her, Mason. Pesky female needs to experience the firm hand of her Alpha."

I raised my eyebrow, crossing my arms over my chest in defiance. "You wouldn't?"

"What? Spank you for breaking the rules of the game? Oh, you know I would." There was a look of hungry intent in his eyes now, and it caused my stomach to flutter. I didn't think there was ever a time I looked at him, and didn't get a wild case of the butterflies.

"You wouldn't do it front of everyone."

He wasn't backing down, and he reached for the bottom of his t-shirt before pulling it off over his head. His body was tight, muscular, and a complete distraction. Everything glistened with sweat, his torso bunched into hard planes and contours, and all I wanted to do was touch it.

He wasn't playing fair.

My brain started to rapidly fire responses. I could taunt him some more and see whether he'd follow through. Or I could play the dutiful werewolf and apologize, promising to be a good girl. Judging from the heat flaring in my own body, we'd be walking a fine line. Having to stay pure until the mating ritual was a challenge in itself, the chemistry between us combustible at times.

"I'm sorry, Mason. Please forgive me." To add proof to my moment of submission, I bowed. "I won't interfere like that again. Promise." I tried to hide the devious smile by bending lower.

"Come on, let's get back to the game," someone in the back yelled.

I looked up at Mason questioningly.

"Your word you'll just play—no goofiness?" He held my gaze.

"I pinky promise." I crooked my little finger at him, wiggling it in invitation as I raised myself to an upright position.

He grabbed my face, crushing his mouth to mine, before releasing me just as quickly. "You make me crazy," he moaned, licking his lips. He turned around and headed to his position.

"Hey, put your shirt back on!" I bent over to pick it up, and tossed the clothing in his direction. "How's a girl to be good if you're distracting her?"

"Figure it out, Darcy. The shirt stays off." He flexed his muscles, hardening his abs before winking cheekily.

"If you're both done with the public display of grossness, let's go," Daniel growled impatiently, and I offered a not very nice gesture to him.

"You're such a lady." He scoffed, but he also nodded. He didn't have to say anything. He loved watching his best friend happy, and I smiled in return.

"Ready to go down?"

"Bring it," he replied.

I tried to play seriously, losing myself in the joy

of being with my family. We were such a close pack, very different from the one I grew up in. Mason had worked hard to build relationships of trust with each member, letting them know they were loved and welcomed. He was an amazing Alpha, and I thanked my lucky stars each day we were to be mated. The transition from my parents pack to this one had been effortless, easing a worry I hadn't known I'd been carrying. I was completely happy, and everything was perfect.

As the afternoon continued, I became bored with being obedient. Jasmine was too, judging from the feigned yawns and looks of annoyance she would flash me. Between the two of us, I was definitely the instigator, and with a final plea, I nodded to her. A wide smile broke across her face, and a renewed burst of energy coursed through her movement. It was time to stir things up, and test Mason's threat of punishment.

My team held possession of the ball, and was in the process of pushing it down the field. The scores were tied, both sides proving their prowess. From the smells in the air, the food had begun to be prepared, so it was crunch time. One of us had to score and steal the game—the perfect opportunity to put my final stunt into action.

The quarterback encircled his arms around the ball, deciding to be the one to run it in, and I watched as bodies came in painful contact with others as they blocked and tackled. There wasn't much room for error, and I gasped in excitement as I watched a space open up.

Moving through it with lightning speed, I mentally urged him forward, beginning to move as well. Mason was there, ready to defend, and everything about his body language told me he would stop the advance. I had to act fast, and make my distraction count. Screaming wouldn't help anymore, but something told me what I contained in my pocket would.

Digging my hand in, wrapping my fingers around the object, I sprinted after the quarterback and threw it with everything I had. I raised my fingers to my mouth, letting out a loud whistle. "There's a flag on the play!"

All movement ceased. We never used penalty markers, so I knew this would confuse them. Both teams started scouring the ground, looking for the piece of material.

There is was. A skimpy piece of lace—my thong to be exact, and Mason's nostrils flared. Others came in for a closer look, and began chuckling loudly, cat calling in appreciation.

I giggled, shrugging my shoulders at Mason as if to say, "Oops." I watched his gaze travel up and down my body. I knew what he was thinking, and I added a slight sway to my hips.

No words left his lips, his burning stare speaking volumes. He charged towards me, throwing me over his shoulder like a fireman, and brought his hand down in a hard, brusque slap on my bottom. Cheers erupted on the field, Jasmine being the loudest.

I tried to break free, but his grip on me was tight. I kicked my legs, finding little leeway as he held them down with his powerful arm. I beat on his back with my fists, and it only caused him to spank again.

"Enough. I was serious, Darcy. Time for your punishment." The ground began to move, and I tilted my head up, trying to figure out where he was taking me. The pack was still standing there, smiling widely over the spectacle. I saw my team's quarterback, and I screamed as loud as I could.

"Make sure you win! Why do you think I did it?" This spurred everyone into action, and noise erupted as my team repeated the play, determined to score the final touchdown. Giving my body one last squirm of resistance, I prepared myself for what would no doubt be an amazing evening.

"I hope you still think that was worth it once I'm done punishing you," Mason murmured, taking me farther away from everyone. My insides melted, and I relaxed into him.

"Promises, promises," I purred. I couldn't stop the wide smile from spreading across my face. He could think he was a big and tough Alpha, but I knew better. He'd been waiting for any excuse to carry me off, eager for some alone time.

He didn't take me far—just out of earshot, but completely hidden from the view of the pack. We didn't have much time as the smell of the BBQ filled the air, and my stomach growled slightly in anticipation. It seemed I'd worked up an appetite, and I was glad someone had seen sense to start it while the game was happening.

Finally letting me down, Mason gave me a few moments to regain my bearings before he started to make his move. He wore a cocky smile, one that screamed he had something in mind for me. I wasn't going to give in too easy though, and for every step he took, I made another backward. He stretched out, only to have me slap his hand away quickly.

"Come on, baby. You have my attention. Wasn't that the whole point behind everything?" He tried to pull me in close, and I was barely able to step out of his reach.

"Of course, but it didn't mean you had to cart me about like a sack of potatoes in front of everyone. You acted like a caveman!" I suppressed the giggle which threatened to break free due to the look on his face.

"I'm no caveman. I'm the Alpha who can do whatever he wants, and right now I want to kiss you." He took another step forward.

"What you need to learn is some manners, Mister. I need to be wooed, not beat over the head and dragged away." I placed my hands on my hips, deciding now was a good time to make a stand because sooner or later, I'd run out of room to maneuver.

"You want to be wooed, huh? I'm not sure I know how to do that. You may have to tell me what to do." The cocky grin he'd been wearing suddenly became softer, his eyes twinkling, and I caught a flash of the boyish charm I'd fallen for.

"Oh no, I'm not explaining anything to you. You should know by now, Mr. Almighty-I-Am-Alpha. Just know this—if you don't get it right ... you're a dead man."

He let out a rich, throaty laugh, and the sound made the soles of my feet tingle. In fact, it made everything tingle, and I braced myself. I was about to get ravished.

I didn't move a muscle as he advanced, or resist as he finally gathered me into his arms. My eyes instantly closed and I tilted my head—waiting. Everything was still, our surroundings dimmed to a quiet hush.

He moved slowly, brushing his mouth against mine softly, tenderly. It was almost like a whisper, the feel of his breath fanning gently over my skin, and when he repeated the motion, goose bumps erupted.

Even though I knew it was coming, the touch of his tongue tracing my bottom lip had me leaning into him, my hands gripping the top of his pants to steady myself. I don't know how long we stood there for, his mouth barely caressing mine before the mood changed, and he made his move.

His arms tightened around me, taking away any chance of escaping, but I wasn't going anywhere. Letting out a sigh of contentment, it was my last thought as I opened my mouth and he swept in, deepening the kiss.

It was nothing short of seductive—the way he dipped and tasted. When I felt his hands slide through my hair, fingers tugging at the loosened strands and releasing it from the ponytail, I moaned and wrapped my arms around his neck. I wanted to anchor myself to him.

My body was thrumming, every part of me alive and basking in Mason's touch. I felt myself weaken, my legs like jelly before he slowly began breaking away. With our mouths only a fraction apart, he leaned in, sucking my lip again into his mouth, his tongue moving for one last loving stroke.

He lowered his head, nuzzling into the crook of my neck. Once he found my sweet spot, he nipped gently, and the sensations shot fiery pulses into my body. He knew what he was doing, proving he understood exactly what I needed. Swirling his tongue to take away the slight sting, he chuckled low.

"So do I live another day, baby?"

It took a moment for me to realize what he was saying, and all I could do was nod.

"Are you going to be okay to go back to the group? By the smell of things, the meal is almost ready."

All I could do was agree again—slow to shake the effects of his kiss.

Taking me by the hand, he led me back to where everyone had started gathering. Tables had been set up, and some of the pack were unfolding chairs. Our appearance was answered with a round of applause and wolf whistles—my disheveled look the source of many comments.

Grinning, I kissed Mason on the cheek and walked over to Jasmine. She was busy moving plates and dishes around on the main table as others were bringing them.

"What do you need me to do?" I asked, moving a stack of cups over so she could place a bowl of potato salad down. "Is there anything more to bring out?"

She began to answer, but one look at me and she burst into laughing. "I see my brother made good use of his time." She lifted her hand, and began to straighten out my hair.

"Of course, just like I knew he would." I couldn't help the confident smile.

"Well, I think we've about got it all done, so you both have perfect timing. We're just waiting for Daniel to finish grilling, and we can all eat."

Looking around the table, I noticed the absence of steak sauce. "You know, the guys are going to throw a fit if they don't have their precious sauce. It may induce a riot," I scoffed, even though there was some truth to my statement. One thing I knew was the pack brothers took their grilling very serious.

"They're just going to have to settle for ketchup then." Jasmine laughed.

"What do we need to settle for?" Daniel interrupted, placing a fresh plate of hot steaks onto the table.

"You're going to need to eat with ketchup today. No problem, right?"

With tongs in one hand, he whipped them around to point at us. "Oh hell yes, there's a problem. Everyone knows you can't use that stuff on your meat. It's practically blasphemous. What are you two ... heathens?" The look of disgust was evident. He looked around for support from the rest of the pack and was answered with a number of agreements. Men.

"Fine then, we'll quickly run into town and grab some before you all die from the inconvenience." I moved away from the table, gesturing Jasmine to follow.

"Where are you going, and why?"

I hadn't heard Mason approaching, and I took in a deep breath. "Daniel seems to think if he doesn't have the right condiment for his meat, it's a travesty, and I'm worried it may scar him permanently." I cast my gaze over at my pack brother, and rolled my eyes again. "So to save his fragile ego, Jasmine and I are going to quickly head to the store to buy some."

"Absolutely not." The tone in his voice said it all—there'd be no argument.

"Do we need to go through this every time I want to go somewhere? I won't be alone, and we'll be back before you know it. You can't keep me under lock and key."

"I'm not trying to, Darcy. I just want to keep you both safe, and my gut says to send someone else for it."

"Ugh, you and your gut." I couldn't finish my sentence, I was so annoyed.

"It's just into town, and the girls will be back before you know it. They're going to keep pestering you until you cave anyway," Daniel interjected, pulling a face.

"Fine, but I'm coming with you then."

"That defeats the purpose! I'm not asking for a lot, just a little independence." I recognized the moment I'd won. Squealing in happiness, I flung my arms around his neck and feathered kisses over his cheek. "I love you. I promise we won't be long."

"Okay, there and back. No side trips." Even though he offered a smile, there was a clear warning in his voice.

Grabbing hold of Jasmine, we made our goodbyes. But before we were out of earshot, I heard Daniel slap Mason on the back.

"Relax, Bro. What's the worst that could happen?"

Chapter Three

We hadn't been in town long when I realized someone was following us. I'd brushed it off as my imagination getting the best of me, but when Jasmine started getting nervous as well, we abandoned our plans, and started heading home.

But whoever was stalking us hadn't given up, and now we were trapped.

The loud click of a gun being cocked stopped me cold. I didn't need to turn around to see death had finally caught us. I closed my eyes for a brief moment and grimaced.

I dug deep for courage as my hand was squeezed. Jasmine would be terrified enough without seeing fear in my eyes and if we were going to get out of this, I needed to keep her calm—or at least calmer than I felt.

Giving her a look I hoped conveyed confidence, I motioned for her to stay quiet as I positioned her behind me and turned to look at our attacker.

I saw the gun, aimed straight at me. The finger poised over the trigger ready to shoot. The hand holding it was steady and trained to adjust to every movement. I shied to the left and back again. Without hesitation, the gun's motion mimicked mine.

Damn. Judging from the precise actions—whoever was holding the gun knew what they were doing. If they took a shot, they wouldn't miss and out running a bullet was too risky.

A quick sniff at the air and drawing on my other senses told me I was dealing with a human male and I couldn't help but grin at the bitter scent of fear mixed in with the sweetness of his excitement. It was intoxicating

My body began to relax. As long as I paid attention to the gun still pointed at me, and made no crazy moves, our chances of escape had just increased.

I looked beyond the weapon and recognized the determined face staring back at me. The emotions rolling off his body caused my wolf to raise her head and howl. This wasn't a pack mate or dominant wolf to play submissive with by showing my throat. Looking at our attacker, I could feel my hackles rise as she growled, desperate to take over.

I sent a silent command to the wolf inside me to stand down. I explained there would be no need for her to come forward because I had everything under control. She whined impatiently at being refused.

Something didn't seem right about the situation. The man standing before me was Gary, and although it caused a slight disturbance in the Pack, he had been declared an official friend.

Without a doubt, Gary knew who Jasmine and I were and our importance. He'd been warned any act of aggression towards the Alpha's intended mate and sister was an instant death sentence – regardless of the person.

My wolf stepped forward again, this time nudging me harder. She sensed the disturbance and it unsettled her. She could smell the danger in the air and begged for permission to take control - to protect us. I could deal with the situation as a wolf, but I was serious when I told Mason to try reasoning before violence. I remembered the last heated discussion between us. He'd laughed when I said we should try to take more peaceful approaches when dealing with conflicts. I didn't always agree with the werewolf mentality of bite first—ask questions later. I'd told him I'd seen too much violence in my life, and was tired of it. When I showed I wouldn't back down, he nodded his approval. I think he got a kick out of the way I stood up to him because our debates always ended up with me pressed up against a surface, Mason kissing me as though he was hungry.

"You don't want to do this, Gary" I spoke, putting as much compulsion in my voice as I could without triggering him. I stepped forward, only to stop when I noticed his eyes darting toward Jasmine. He held a crazed look, and I needed his focus away from her.

"Don't assume to know what I want," he spat out, spittle flying from his lips.

My mind raced. Mentally cringing, I remembered my last words to Mason. "You don't need to come with us every time we leave the house. There's no threat. We'll be back soon." That had been my intentions but when I sensed someone following, I'd tried to evade them, but with no luck, unable to leave and get back to pack property. Searching for somewhere private to hide until the danger had passed, I wanted to laugh because my brilliant plan had clearly bitten us in the butt. I hadn't saved us at all. We were now trapped between freedom and a madman with a gun.

Mentally I crossed my fingers as I assessed the situation, hoping this would be another case of me escaping by the skin of my teeth with no harm done.

Jasmine's exhale of breath drove home the seriousness of the moment. I knew she was scared, and I needed to get us out of here.

I took in Gary's expression and noticed the trickle of sweat rolling down the sides of his cheek. The man may have nerves of steel when it came to handling weapons, but he wasn't as unaffected as he let on. Judging by the slight tick in his right eye and the way he kept licking his lips, he was nervous and I could use that to my advantage.

My brain scrambled for what I knew of him. Mason had asked Gary last summer to help with the home renovations he'd planned. Even though they had little in common, there was something about the human which endeared him to the Alpha, and he started including Gary in certain Pack activities.

I wondered what triggered him. Something had pushed him over the edge and made him lose control. I wasn't sure how to handle the situation because causing Gary to freak out would make him fire the gun. If I launched myself at him, my werewolf strength might overpower him and knock him out. Or I could be patient and see if talking my way out this helped. Either choice was a gamble. Right now he called all the shots and that left very little wiggle room for me to act.

I knew there was two sure fire ways to get a response out of a man – turn him on or piss him off, and judging by how my pack brothers carried on, I figured turning Gary on would be the easiest way to resolve this.

My plan was I'd bat my eyelids, toss in a pouty smile, and flirt the gun right out of his grip. I knew the effect I had on men when I turned on the charm, the way they became putty in my hands. People joked how Mason governed the Pack with an iron fist but all I had to do was crook my little finger and he'd come running. I would need all my confidence to pull this off because the very thought I'd have to touch him made my skin crawl. My stomach tossed about as I offered a silent prayer.

Men respond to a third thing, my wolf growled as she paced beneath the surface. Violence.

She craved to be let loose so she could pounce on Gary and eliminate him. She was blood thirsty and enraged, and I struggled to control the feral energy she gave off. I needed to keep her restrained because there wasn't a chance in hell he'd survive her attack.

I took in a deep breath, desperate to release the tension in my muscles. I had to move with grace if I was to play the role of the seductress.

I felt my lips curve into a smile as I lifted my arm to touch him. I forced my hands to look soft and not curl into claws to rip out his throat. Lowering my voice, I whispered, "Come now Gary, there must be something we can do to move past this. You don't want to hurt me." I let my other hand roll down the length of my body, hoping to keep his attention.

His focus remained on my face, and panic flickered in his eyes before he hid it. But I'd caught it. He didn't like what I was doing. He was becoming anxious and I could work with that.

"You need to stop whatever it is you're doing," his voice came out in a rushed puff.

I closed the distance between us, never taking my eyes off him. Digging deep to steady my hands, I caressed the side of his cheek, making sure I continued to breath in and out. He hadn't shaved, the stubble feeling coarse under my fingertips.

My wolf growled, fighting hard for dominance. She didn't like this, but I couldn't let her out. She nipped at me, showing her displeasure and I struggled to ignore her.

Bile rose up into my mouth as my fingers traced

41

over his cheekbones. "See, we can work this out, Gary. There's no need for violence." I wanted to add he could put the gun down, but I didn't want to remind him he had it.

I pressed my body against his. His eyes instantly widened, pupils dilating.

Leaning in, I purred into his ear. "Is there somewhere we can go? Maybe a little more private? Let Jasmine leave, Gary. We don't need her."

I forced my other hand to rest on his chest for a moment before it began to journey downward, making sure to let out small moans of appreciation as if touching him pleased me. It felt like bitter ash on my tongue and all I could think of was the long, hot shower I would need to scrub his scent off me. If it was even possible

He didn't move a fraction, remaining stiff, his arm still stretched out with the gun now aimed at Jasmine. I couldn't tell how receptive he was based on his body language.

"You need to stop," the words exploded out of his mouth through clenched teeth. "What kind of idiot do you think I am? You are the alpha's mate, his most beloved, and you expect me to believe you want me?" Scorn and disbelief dripped heavily off his words, and I lost my hold over him as his anger rose to the surface.

"Shhhh," I tried to bring Gary's focus back to me as I moved face to face with him, my mouth a breath away from his. His lips felt dry against mine, and I fought the urge to lick my lips to moisten them.

"What Mason doesn't know won't hurt him. You can't tell me you're not curious about what it's like to be with a werewolf." I lowered my voice to a sultry tone. "The heat that's created. Not knowing what's woman and what's animal. They say it's quite the experience."

I could faintly hear Jasmine behind me, and I tried

not to think what this looked like. She was loyal to her brother and even though she knew this was an act, it mustn't be sitting well with her.

I couldn't sense if her wolf had risen. Thank goodness for small miracles. I was having a hard enough time keeping mine corralled without dealing with a second one.

The rankness of Gary's breath reached my nose, reminding me of my purpose. It reeked of cheap liquor and something else, a familiar smell. The scent triggered a red flag in my mind.

Gary had laced his liquid courage. It was so elusive, like it was on the tip of my tongue but I couldn't quite remember. There was an otherworldly smell to his breath and it hinted at magic. When my brain finally finished figuring it out, I was stunned.

Vampire. The fool had drunk vampire blood.

A pulse of fear washed over me, leaving an icy trail through my body that caused my skin to pebble and break into a light sweat. Here I was, thinking I was dealing with a mere human, but with this extra boost, I had no idea what could happen.

I stood, hovered over his lips, my hand on his abdomen, my mind searching for my next move. So far, he hadn't fallen for my act and time was running out. I needed to go all in and finish this.

Adding a wriggle to my stance, I reached for his belt buckle and pulled his body hard against mine. I wrapped my other arm around his back, pressing my chest to his. At the same time, I nipped at his lower lip to let him know I wanted access to his mouth. As his lips parted, my tongue dove in and I gagged as the rancid flavor of his breath touched my taste buds. I stumbled forward, but quickly recovered and applied myself more to the vomit inducing kiss.

The feel of the gun's cold metal at my temple was unmistakable, and my body stiffened.

I'd just willingly put myself into his hands because he hadn't been fooled at all by my ruse. A quick inhale through my nose told me the fear I'd been able to smell on him earlier had morphed into arrogance.

Gary's deep chuckle resonated through him, chilling my blood instantly, and I felt myself sag a little.

Everything changed, and my wolf howled in triumph, knowing I'd have to accept the inevitable— sooner or later I was going to have to release her.

Gary ground the barrel of the gun hard into my skin, a reminder of who was in charge. In a move I could only attribute to the vampire blood in him, he turned me around, and he faced me toward Jasmine. His arms circled my chest, crushing me.

Jasmine looked horrified as a steady stream of tears flowed down her cheeks. She appeared deathly pale and her body trembled.

She was too young to witness something like this— we both were. Violence amongst the pack was one thing, but senseless violence at the end of a gun was another.

I tried to move, twisting hard in his grip but it only made him tighten his arm, and for a moment I couldn't breathe as his embrace constricted my lungs. I continued to struggle, trying to find a way to break free. There wasn't a weakness. Gary's strength matched mine.

"Shhhh, what Mason doesn't know won't hurt him," Gary taunted, mocking me with my own words. My knees gave out as I felt his slippery tongue trail a path on my skin, licking me from the base of my neck to my ear in one slimy motion.

Jasmine cleared her throat, and I saw her step

forward, the beginnings of anger on her face. Her wolf was beginning to break through and assert herself. Great.

I raised my hand to stop her, pleading with my eyes as I mouthed for her to stay where she was.

"Oh by all means, come forward Jasmine. It's actually you I'm here for." Gary's low chuckle rang in my ear. "You didn't think it was you, Darcy? No, I've had my eye on Jasmine for a long time. I'm going to get what I want."

Confusion hit me. Scene after scene from the last few months played through my mind as I tried to make some kind of connection. There had been numerous times when Jasmine and Gary were together, but never alone and not once had I sensed any attraction—especially on Jasmine's side.

We were close and told each other everything. If she was falling in love with this man, I would've known about it.

Jasmine's eyes widened in shock from the declaration and even though I knew I couldn't move, it didn't stop me from wanting to comfort her.

"What do you want with her?"

Gary's arm tightened slightly as he adjusted his stance. "I want her as my mate, or whatever it is you freaks call it, but Mason said no. All summer long, I've been trying to show what a decent guy I am and because I'm not a wolf, I didn't even stand a chance." It was impossible to miss the bitter anger as his voice rang out.

"I tried convincing Mason it didn't matter, that I would treat her well and follow any pack rules he wanted, but that animal ...." Gary paused to draw an angry breath, and my wolf bristled at the tone being used. "Mason wouldn't hear any of it. Kept apologizing to me and saying it wasn't the way things were done. He had someone else in mind for his sister, but hoped we could still be friends. Friends!" Spit flew from behind me at the force of his last word. "We will never be friends."

"Gary, pack marries pack. Mason is right ...." I was silenced by the gun smashing hard against the side of my head. My wolf practically bounced off my skin in an attempt to break free over the quick act of aggression.

"I don't care about your stupid pack or its archaic rules. They mean nothing to me. I love her and I will have her—whatever it takes."

"But vampires? You went to vampires?" I knew I was tempting my fate but I couldn't keep the incredulous tone from my voice. Gary relaxed a little as he took in a breath to speak.

"I was desperate. Depressed. They found me and offered me a way to get her."

"Yeah, but at the cost of your soul!" I exclaimed. "No one is worth that."

He moved so quickly. One minute I had my back to him and next his hand was locked around my throat, in a death grip, the barrel of the gun resting between my eyes.

"Say it again, I dare you. Say Jasmine isn't worth it, and I'll splatter your brains all over the ground." Gary's eyes were crazed, and I knew I'd pushed him too far. There'd be no reaching him. One of us was going to die.

We stared into each other's eyes, willing the other to relent. A firm voice broke our concentration. "Let her go, Gary. It's me you want, and I promise I'll go with you. Just stop this madness."

Gary released me to look at Jasmine, suspicious hope on his face. I dropped to the floor, gasping for air with my hand massaging my throat. I'd give this to the human—he had an iron strong grip.

"Leave us alone, Gary. Please," Jasmine growled.

It was the please that drew my attention. There was a hint of animal in the sound, and my stomach dropped as I watched Jasmine fight to rein in her wolf. It was relentlessly trying to gain control now, the trauma of the evening triggering it to break free and surface.

The situation just went from dangerous to dire. Judging from the convulsions racking her body, we were going to have a real problem in a moment. Scratch that. Gary was about to have a problem, and my wolf howled in anticipation.

"You need to calm down, Jasmine. Take deep breaths. Everything's alright," I spoke softly, watching her carefully. "Just try to keep your body relaxed and mind focused. Okay? Don't give in, fight to stay human."

Gary reached down and grabbed me by my jacket, dragging me to my feet. "What's happening? What's wrong with her?" He used the gun to point at Jasmine, who had dropped to all fours—panting heavily.

"She's changing, you idiot I need to get her out of here." I used my hands to roughly shove at Gary. "Let me go now!" I threw every ounce of compulsion into my voice. I didn't care what his issues were, Jasmine needed me and that was all that mattered.

"No! No Mason. Just you. Fix her." The gun's trigger clicked back on as he aimed it at me. "Now."

I lost my temper. I thought nothing about diplomacy or trying to ease the weapon out of his hand. It didn't matter he seemed just as on edge as I was. Jasmine's whimpers were becoming louder and louder as the change began to take over.

"There's no fixing her! This is who and what she is – she's a werewolf, and if I can't stop her changing, she may not be able to hold onto her humanity. Do you get it, you jerk? Your macho act of stupidity here ...." I pointed at his gun, "has triggered her wolf. She'll be too strong to fight and will take control—maybe forever."

I ran over to where Jasmine was lying. She was now in the fetal position, lying on her side, and I could see her muscles and joints starting to lengthen and rearrange themselves. Her nails had grown longer, sharper at the tips and a light coat of fur rippled and flashed over her skin. Most times the Change occurred faster, but as she struggled against it, it seemed to take forever.

"Come on, Jasmine. Fight it." I groped my pockets for my cell phone and cursed out aloud. Of course, this would be the time I left it at home.

I began a silent chant in my head for Mason, trying to send a frantic call through the pack bond. I repeated my message over and over, sending images—hoping something was getting thorough.

"I can sense her, Darcy, and she's desperate to get out. She feels so strong this time, and I'm scared I won't be able to hold on to me when she comes." Fear blazed in her wolfish eyes. The yellow tint almost glowed in darkness of the evening.

"Do you remember what they taught us to do if this ever happened? About how as you feel your wolf pass, to focus on what makes you Jasmine? Tell me what you're going to think about?"

"I'm going to think ...." Her thought was cut short as a gut wrenching scream erupted from her mouth. The press of the gun barrel returned to the side of my head.

"Enough with your damn gun, Gary. Enough!" My own wolf, hungry for action, felt that much closer.

"What's happening? Make it stop! It's not supposed to be like this. I meant to kidnap her, whisk her away where I could have a chance to win her over, make her see she could love me. I wanted to get her away from pack and all things wolf, and we would've been happy."

The arrogant facade Gary had been maintaining started to crumble as hysteria crept into his voice. He drove his hand through his hair and began to pace back and forth, the gun still in his grip.

"Just take your gun and walk away. Mason will arrive soon, and you're not going to want to be here when I tell him what happened. Forget about Jasmine—about us all. Just leave!" I screamed the last words at him as I used my hands to try and soothe Jasmine.

"No, I'm not leaving without what I came for. Fix her, and we'll leave together."

I almost choked on my shock. This guy was truly delusional if he thought I was letting him anywhere near Jasmine again. Standing to my feet, I turned to face Gary and stalked toward him.

"You'll go, and you'll go now before I rip your throat out. I've had enough of this. You're wasting my time. Don't make me do something I'll regret." I shoved him and pointed to down the street. "Run, while you can. You think Jasmine will be scary? You have no idea what it's like to face an infuriated alpha wolf and pack members. You have no idea what it'll be like facing me."

The sound of a wolf growling behind me interrupted my angry rant. I closed my eyes, not needing to turn around to know she'd changed, and from the electricity dancing over my skin and the tension beneath it, it wouldn't be long before I'd change as well.

"Run, I will not warn you again!"

A look of revulsion crossed over Gary's face. I turned around to face Jasmine, and it didn't take a genius to see he didn't like what he saw. His reaction was confusing because this was nature at its finest.

Jasmine was a breathtaking wolf – silver fur with white tipped ears and paws. Her snout was ebony and her fur shined in the moonlight.

"Make her change back!" he screeched.

I reached out with my senses to see whether I could find her, but I was too distracted by what was happening around me. "I don't know if I can. I don't know if she's there. Mason will have to help her. She needs her Alpha."

I took a step towards Jasmine, with my hands raised in a submissive gesture. Technically, we were the same in the hierarchy of the Pack, I wouldn't rise until Mason and I had officially sealed our mate bond. I hoped my showing her I meant no threat, she would calm enough for me to reach her. Her hackles were still raised, and there was a low grumble coming from her, but it was directed at Gary more. Jasmine would smell I was part of the Pack, whether she was herself or not and know I wasn't a threat.

"Don't go near her!"

"Make your mind up, Gary! You either want me to help her or not." I was getting sick of his interference, sick of his presence, and I was ready to snap. Play time was over, and it was time to put end to this.

Using my werewolf speed, I turned and lunged for Gary, baring my teeth at him. I caught him by surprise and quickly had him pinned beneath me on the floor. I wrestled for control of the gun and misjudged a move. A second later, I was underneath Gary, with his fist pummeling into my face.

A loud howl echoed and was followed by an angry

growl of warning. Gary turned to see Jasmine launch herself at his back. He raised the gun and fired.

Chapter Four

The shot thundered and time seemed to stop. All I could hear was my shallow breathing and the sound of a body thudding to the ground.

"Nooooo!" An agonizing scream erupted from my throat as I pushed the shell shocked Gary off me and scrambled over to where Jasmine now lay—still in wolf form.

A pool of blood was steadily forming underneath her, and my fingers frantically tried to find where the bullet entered so I could stop the bleeding. All I could see was fur and gore as tears blurred my vision.

I lowered my head down to the wolf's body and could hear Jasmine's heart slowly giving out. She seemed to shudder a little as if her body was trying to rally one more time before she was finally still. Even with supernatural abilities to heal, there was only so much her body could do.

"Don't you dare die, Jasmine. Fight!" I started to shake her, but had to stop as the change reversed itself. In the event of death, anyone who passed away in wolf form would revert back to their human selves. As I rolled Jasmine to her back, I administered C.P.R.

Was it thirty compressions and two breathes, or two breathes and fifteen compressions? I couldn't remember. My brain wasn't able to calm itself long enough to remember.

A memory pierced the moment. "It's better to

55

do something than nothing, Darcy. Do what you can." It was the voice of an old instructor advising me after I'd asked what to do if I forgot.

I began pushing down in the middle of her sternum, not stopping when I heard one of her ribs pop. I kept repeating the numbers over and over in my mind like a mantra.

Nothing was happening. Jasmine continued to lie still on the ground, as each moment passed becoming colder and colder, her body's heat leaving. Hysteria threatened to explode from me.

I would've kept working on her if I hadn't heard a noise behind me. I was so focused on saving the life of my beloved friend and future sister, I'd forgotten about Gary.

Part of me hoped he'd taken my advice and left. My wolf, she hoped he'd stayed. Grief tormented her, and she demanded justice for the death of her fellow pack mate. She begged to be released so she could execute him, and in my weakened state, I took down the walls and set her free.

I tried to do this the civilized way, and it ended in disaster. I should've let her out at the very beginning, letting her destroy the threat. If I had, Jasmine and I would be on our way home right now, laughing about ways to torture Mason.

I took a deep breath as I leaned forward and closed Jasmine's eyes. I kissed her softly on cheek and whispered I'd be back for her.

Something within me finally snapped, my wolf was in full control. Placing my hands on the floor to push myself up, I turned to face my enemy.

The gun was on the ground a few feet away, useless. The enemy stood a short distance away, shaking from shock as he stared at Jasmine in disbelief.

He didn't have the right to look at her. He had no

right to even breathe, and if I had anything to do with it, he wouldn't be in a few short moments.

I took a measured step forward, power soaking my cells as I called on the change to happen. "You will pay for this." My voice was an octave deeper, but steady as a rock, as I sized up my enemy. "You killed her so your life is forfeit. So says pack law." I felt my face harden. "I told you to stop. You didn't. I told you to run yet you stayed. Because of you, my sister is now dead. Run as fast as your vampire blood laced body can, because when I catch you, you'll wish you'd never been born."

"It was an accident, Darcy. I didn't mean to shoot her. I loved her! I never meant for this to happen." My enemy was frantic and began to back up slowly.

He mimicked the submissive gestures I'd shown Jasmine earlier. His hands held up in peace, but there would be none now. The wolf was here, and she was without mercy.

I took another step forward and jerked as my muscles and joints moved. It had been slow and painful for Jasmine, but Mason and I had been working on my changes. As the mate of the Alpha, he told me there would be times I'd be challenged and it was important I could change fast and often. If my enemy thought he had more time, he was sorely mistaken.

"You really should've run" And with that, a savage pulse pushed through my body. One minute I was Darcy and next I wasn't.

Standing in all my wolfish glory, I saw my enemy cower as he watched me change into two hundred pounds of aggression and raw energy. I may not be as spectacular as Jasmine, but my chocolate brown fur was thick and luxurious, my fangs sharp and eager to shred.

My humanity whispered in my head, trying to convince me against attacking, but my grief held too tight a grip. Somewhere else inside, I could feel Mason was close by, but I shut the sensation off too. This was personal and something I wanted to deal with. By killing Jasmine, my enemy had crossed a line human Darcy couldn't argue with. Pack dictated retribution, and the thrill of it set my senses ablaze.

I stalked toward my enemy as it backed up, looking over its shoulder for help. Hoping for privacy to enact its kidnap, it had gotten just that, but it also meant no one would be coming to its defense now. No one would hear it scream in terror.

I faked a lunge, and it squeaked in terror. Head back, I howled, the noise jolting the enemy before me. It finally turned and ran.

My enemy became prey.

I paced back and forth eagerly, allowing it a few moments head start before leaping into action. Barking out a war cry, I loped after it, careful not to catch my prey too quickly. I wanted to draw out the uncertainty—torture it.

Down the street I chased, pausing to test the scent on the air. I knew exactly where it was, but also smelled the pack. They wouldn't get here in time. Even if they did, this was my kill—my death sentence to execute.

I skidded to a halt at the opening of an alleyway. Instead of running into a populated area, or flagging down a passing car, my prey chose to hide where there could be no escape.

If it thought the filth which littered the ground could disguise its fear riddled odor, it was about to be disappointed. The trash crunched under my feet as I entered the space and stood for a moment, taking in my surroundings.

I ignored the rats rummaging around. Howling out the equivalent of "ready or not, here I come," and slowly began stalking. It took only a second to narrow down where the coward was hiding—a boarded over doorway. Its sweat drenched body radiated a "here I am" sign. I crouched down and waited.

Moments passed. Silence filled the air. I wanted it to think danger had passed it by, and everything was safe. I wanted it to relax before I pounced and ripped it apart. Slowly.

Cautiously, I saw it begin to move, testing each movement for a reaction. When it seemed appeased, my prey stood up and peered into the alley way, scanning the area. It relaxed, releasing the tense breath it had been holding, and as it stepped out I growled. I snapped at the strangled response as my prey jumped back into its hiding spot. The smell of urine was strong as it wet itself.

Stalking to the opening of the doorway, anger and retribution drenching me, I faced the cowering lump in front of me. I could drag this out, make it suffer more, or I could end it.

Springing from my hind legs, I soared through the air and landed on top of it. With a feral bark, I demanded it look at me.

Recognition of its impending death filled its eyes, and my prey mouthed a silent prayer—a plea for divine intervention. Pouncing, my paws dug into its chest, pinning it to the floor. I leaned in to take one last sniff.

This is for Jasmine, I shouted as I opened my jaws and ripped at its body. Blood sprayed over the walls and into my mouth. Sounds of shredding flesh and limbs being brutally torn from the body filled the air, as well as the heady scent of copper.

Agonizing screams followed, but it meant nothing as I focused on annihilating the pack enemy. With one quick move, I ripped its throat out—silencing it forever.

It didn't take long before it ceased moving, and there was nothing left but carnage—blood and gore covering every surface. I stopped long enough to shake out my body, sending bits of flesh flying from my fur.

Nudging the lifeless mass with my snout, I growled a challenge for it to get up and fight some more. There was no movement.

Adrenaline still coursed through my body, but it was over. Justice had been served, with a side of ruthless vengeance, and it was time to change back.

I reached inside and called on the change, but my wolf refused to relinquish control.

I pushed, and she pushed harder.

I begged and coerced. She ignored it all.

It was then I panicked. It had been a long time since the wolf had been this strong, and there was no budging her. She was adamant if she had been in control to begin with, this all could've been avoided. We were to stay wolf, and everyone would be safe.

Realizing I couldn't reason with her at the moment, I began the journey back to Jasmine's body. She'd been concealed so I hoped no one had discovered her and moved her.

My slow steps became huge bounding lopes as I pushed myself to get back to where it had all started.

Nearing the scene, my hackles rose, and I let out a warning growl. Some of the pack had arrived and were hovering over Jasmine's body. I barked for them to move as I roughly pushed my way through those who'd come. Daniel. Jonas. Eric.

The looks on their faces were a mixture of anger, grief, and shock. Violence was something mostly seen amongst the dominant pack members. It was rare for it to touch the females, so the death of Jasmine would shake them to the core.

Each of them looked at me cautiously, trying not to make eye contact as they assessed the situation. They could see my aggression, hear it in my low growls, and tried to show they weren't a threat.

Crouched over the body of his sister was Mason, his head bowed as silent sobs wracked his body. I longed to comfort him but couldn't as a wolf.

I nudged him with my snout, ignoring the blood stain I left on his t-shirt. His hand reached out and ruffled through my fur. It came back sticky.

"Hi baby, you okay?" He gave me the once over, waiting to see how I would react to him. I leaned in slowly, taking my time to pull his scent into my lungs.

Mason sat still, and a feeling of security washed over me. I nudged him again. He threw his arm around me, pulling me in close.

I could feel his strength permeating into my body, trying to soothe away my anger. I began to whimper, trying to tell him all that happened as my body shuddered against him.

"I can't understand you, Darcy. You're going to need to change back. We need to move Jasmine and get back to the house. Come on, sweetheart, as soon as you're ready." He gestured with one of his hands to Eric and Daniel, and they moved forward to pick up Jasmine.

Instantly my wolf reacted, and I nipped at them. Standing guard over my fallen sister's body, I forced them to back up—Mason included. No one was going to touch her, not until we could figure out how to bring her back. My grief demanded it.

"Darcy, you can let go and change back. No one is going to hurt Jasmine. Eric and Daniel need to pick her up so we can take her home. She needs the pack. She needs the rituals."

Everything he said made sense. I just couldn't let go of the belief if we waited a little longer, she'd wake up—alive.

The guys moved to step forward again and this time, I lashed out biting at the pant leg of Daniel.

"Darcy. Stand down." The Alpha command battered against me, ruthless in its primal demand. No one could resist it, but I tried anyway.

"She's fighting it!" Jonas exclaimed in shock. "Look at her. She's got a hard set in her eyes, Mason. I don't think she's going to listen."

"Darcy. Don't make me force you." Mason ordered, sadness filling his eyes. Pure Alpha compulsion coated my body and soaked into my bones, forcing me to relax. Pain caused me to yelp as I struggled to hold my position. I didn't want them touching her.

"Darcy!" and with that one word, I crumbled. Eric and Daniel quickly stepped in, sweeping Jasmine up. As I watched them carry her away to the waiting car, I released a grief stricken howl that began in my stomach, and erupted from my mouth into the night.

On and on I howled, understanding all hope had been futile. She truly was gone, and the only "magic" ritual to perform now would be a burial one. I collapsed to the floor and buried my snout into my paws.

I barely heard the voices whispering. Footsteps came and went, followed by the sound of a car engine starting and the vehicle pulling away. Everyone had left—all but Mason, his hand gently stroking my fur. There was a soothing rhythm to his movement, but my wolf was far from being calmed.

I don't know how long we sat there or why we

weren't found. I didn't care. Nothing mattered anymore, and nothing made sense.

His voice jolted me to awareness. "You're not able to change back, are you? Is that why you're still in wolf form? She won't let go?"

I raised my head and looked into concerned eyes. Mason lifted his hand and gently stroked the fur on my face, each touch filled with love. I nodded slightly, the best I could do to communicate with him. I knew this was serious—I needed to regain control, but didn't know how to convince my wolf it was okay.

"Well as Alpha, I can force the change. I'm worried if I do though, the wolf will resent me, and I don't want it coming between us. We could wait and see if she relents, but something tells me tonight was too traumatic, and she sees this as a matter of survival for you both."

Mason paused, looking thoughtful as he studied the problem out. I marveled at how amazing he was. He knew exactly what was happening, and it not only spoke volumes about the type of leader he was, it showed the kind of man he was as well. He was my mate, and it filled me with a sense of security to know this was the man who would swear to love and protect me for the rest of my life.

A thought popped into my head at the same time a smile spread over his face. The light sparkling in his eyes told me he had an idea and believed it would work.

"I know how we can convince her to release you. She's always been there to protect you, keep you safe and out of harm's way. It's a natural response, but she needs to realize there's another who can do that for you as well—someone who wants to and is ready to step in. She needs to relinquish control over to me as your mate."

Relief coursed through me as Mason shared the same idea I'd had, and something in my gut told me this was the answer. Who better to keep me safe at the moment and in the future than my mate? Even my wolf couldn't argue too long with that.

I felt her respond to the idea and stubbornly acknowledge that maybe Mason was right. She still needed a little convincing though. She wasn't going to hand over anything just yet.

I didn't understand the hesitancy. He was a good man and wolf. I'd seen Mason in action and so had my wolf. What she was waiting for was beyond me.

I looked at him again—trying to share what was happening and got up to sit on my haunches as he quickly pulled away. His body began to shimmer and pulse.

He was changing. It was one of those blink and you miss it kind of deals. One minute Mason was sitting there, and the next a magnificent wolf.

I would never tire of looking at him—if there was ever the poster child for werewolves, Mason was it. All sleek curves and muscles, he was the color of midnight, perfect for blending into the darkness.

His black fur was immaculate and covered every inch of his perfectly formed body. With strong legs and finely tuned agility, he was a lethal predator and competition to all who crossed his path.

And he was all mine.

With a quick shake, he padded over and prodded me with his nose. When I didn't move and tilted my head in question, he nudged me again. Let her look, a voice echoed in my mind and I understood. If my wolf was going to release control, she needed to see and approve of who would also be protecting me.

I jumped up onto my paws, pushing at my stubborn

wolf and showed her Mason's wolf. Even she couldn't deny he was glorious, and I begged for her to take a closer look.

Standing at attention, waiting for inspection, Mason's wolf didn't flinch as I began to nip and poke at him. Rubbing my body against his, energy emanated off of him, and caused my own to sizzle from the contact. Energy like that meant only one thing—power and lots of it.

My wolf nodded at the feel of it and approached the front of our mate. Without warning, she growled and barked at him, baring her fangs as she set back in a pounce like stance. She was preparing to attack. I screamed for her to stop. We don't attack our mates, but she wouldn't listen.

He stood stoically, never flinching as she launched at him. Landing on top of him, he let my body pin him to the ground as my wolf snarled and snapped. She was provoking an attack on purpose, wanting to see his reaction.

A rough tongue whipped out, licking the side of my snout. Seconds later, Mason's wolf tilted his head and bared his throat—a sign of submission. Instantly, the fighting instinct fled, and I began to change. Mason had passed her test.

It took only moments before I felt myself being scooped up into strong arms. Mason's scent wafted over me, and I couldn't help taking in a deep breath. After all I'd been through, it spoke of comfort, and I wanted to submerge myself in it.

Everything was quiet except for the sound of our breathing, still slightly labored from our changes. For a moment, it was as if everything was okay and then the crushing weight of reality bore down and threatened to bury me alive.

"Oh my gosh, Mason. Jasmine ...." I couldn't

finish my sentence as a sob ripped from me. It was impossible to hold back the barrage of emotions washing over me as tears streamed down my face.

Over and over I cried. He gently rocked me back and forth, not speaking a word as he joined me in my grief. My sadness knew no end, and I felt like I was drowning as the events of the night replayed themselves in my mind.

"Oh no, Mason. I ripped him to shreds!" Vomit forced itself up my throat, and I was barely able to pull myself free before it violently erupted out of my mouth. I could feel my hair being held back as my stomach emptied itself. I continued to heave even though there was nothing left—like I was trying to purge the events from my body.

When I finally settled, I wiped the back of my hand over my face and glanced back at Mason. He looked haggard, the worry and strain of tonight clearly written on his expression. Love shone from his eyes, as well as deep anguish over the death of his sister.

"Take me home please. I want to go to sleep so when I wake up I can say this was all a dream. That's what this is right, it's just a dream?" I begged for him to lie to me, to tell me anything but the truth.

"We'll talk about it when you wake up, okay? Here, let me help you." Scooping under my legs, Mason tenderly lifted me into his arms again. "Sleep Darcy, you're safe. I have you now."

My wolf howled in agreement, and I felt my body slowly begin to relax. Hesitating for a moment, I closed my eyes, and it wasn't long before the blessed blanket of sleep embraced me. My last thought, Please, let this be a dream.

Chapter Five

A deafening blast broke the silence and dragged me screaming through the choking darkness. Gasping for breath, frantically seeking for something to cling to, I faltered for a moment when I found the space beside me empty. I struggled to focus, my hands restlessly moving about, but there was nothing. That's when the terror began to pull me back under.

Flashes of images, so shocking, fired rapidly at me. They were jumbled at first, but slowly they began to make sense, and it came with a gut wrenching pain that stole my breath. Suddenly, my ears were filled with the fury laden howl of a wolf. My wolf. She was furious and in no way consolable. The nightmare had triggered memories in her also.

My heart raced, beating hard against my chest, and I let out a strangled whimper as I fought to regain control. Closing my eyes, I tried to block out the thoughts bombarding me as the events of the night began to replay themselves. Without realizing, I started to rock back and forth.

Jasmine. Beautiful, sweet, perfect Jasmine. Gone, and it was all my fault. It was my stubborn pride—thinking I could protect us, which had led to the fateful encounter. It was because of my inability to act that I couldn't stop him from stealing her from me.

Bile rose in my throat, bringing with it a taste that caused my wolf to suddenly stop her howling. A new feeling surged through me, one of triumph and a strong sense of retribution. She was pleased with her part in the evening, and I couldn't help the shudders overtaking my body as I connected the unique flavor filling my mouth.

Flesh and blood. His. I couldn't hide away from the small sense of satisfaction I felt. Even though I hadn't been able to take care of it, she had. She'd taken a firm hold of the situation, pushed me into the background, and hunted the monster down. Without mercy. Without hesitation.

Tearing him limb from limb until he was unrecognizable, she refused to give back control, adamant she was the only way to keep us safe. Looking down at my body as it nestled under piles of soft, warm blankets, I strained to remember how I managed to convince her to release me.

A name whispered in my mind, and my muscles instantly relaxed as if the mere mention of him was enough to ease the tension. Mason. He had come, and his help had restored me. He'd seen the devastation, how I'd failed him, and still he had patiently been there.

Shame pounded into me. How could I possibly look him in the eye again, knowing I cost him his beloved sister? Sure, he brought me back, but it was more from the duty of being the Alpha, and I doubted he would still want to mate with me.

Just the idea of never completing the bond stirred up fear and an agony so acute, tears began to stream down my face. I pulled my knees up into my chest and hugged them, continuing my steady rocking.

What am I going to do?

Thoughts raced through my mind and I could feel the hysteria building. The nightmare had finally released me from its grip, but now a new one, a world without Jasmine, Mason, and my pack began to take shape, and it was by far the most terrifying.

A noise erupted into the air, disturbing the silence of the room. It took a moment to realize I was the one making it. I was shocked to hear how weak and destitute I sounded. There was nothing confident about it. It belonged to someone who had just lost everything, and the weight of it crushed me.

I clamped a hand over my mouth, desperate to stop the noise before it brought people to my room. The last thing I needed was everyone trying to figure out what happened. It would come soon enough if I knew the rumor mill at all. I was part of a pretty amazing pack, the Mystic Wolves, but like most, we enjoyed a little gossip, and I wasn't ready to face it.

Another thought shot through my mind, one that made me wince. I can't let anyone see me like this. Vulnerable and weak. Being almost mated to the Alpha came with authority and a position of pride amongst the pack—a greatly coveted position for those looking to advance. I'd made sure to maintain friendly relationships with everyone, but who knew when someone would get it in their head to throw down the gauntlet.

Maybe that's the best thing. Have someone challenge me and let them win. It would solve everyone's problem. Even before the thought was completed, it made me choke. Yes, things felt dire at the moment, but this wasn't me. I wasn't a wolf to just lie down and bare my throat without a fight. I may feel like a failure, but I would never do something so cowardly—so unbecoming and faint-hearted.

No, I need to just leave. Get out of bed, pack a few things, and go into hiding. Mason will eventually forget me and stop looking. If I run far enough, maybe I can start again.

My wolf growled at the idea, showing me just how distasteful my musings were. Mason had reached her earlier and she was now fiercely loyal to him. She didn't want to hear any nonsense about leaving. Besides, she warned me, Mason would never stop looking, and he'd bring in other packs to help. The only way to avoid that was to go rogue, and the idea bristled against my pride. I was too much of a "pack" girl to ever go it alone.

What am I going to do?

You're going to stop thinking and just let me hold you, a voice as warm as melted chocolate echoed through my mind and slid over my body. I stopped my rocking and opened my eyes, looking for the source.

"Mason?"

I'm here. Just waiting and watching.

A rustle from the corner of the room drew my attention, and I found him—the man who made my heart sing and dance, sitting on the floor with his back against the wall. A closer look showed he was still in the same clothes from yesterday, giving him a crumpled look I couldn't deny was sexy. Each time I looked at him, it stole my heart, and it hurt to know I'd lost him.

"What are you doing down there? Something wrong with the chair?" I looked over to the plush armchair I had everyone drag in for me, and I instantly saw the problem—it was covered with piles of unfolded clothes. Being a procrastinator, I'd never got around to putting them away.

"I wanted you to rest, but couldn't bring myself to leave. You tossed and turned a lot."

Speaking aloud, Mason's voice had the same effect over me. To some, he just sounded like an ordinary guy, but as a werewolf I could feel the authority and power flowing through it. I could also hear his weariness and sorrow.

"You didn't want to share my bed?" I couldn't believe how small I sounded as I spoke my fears. It hurt knowing he found me so repulsive he'd rather sit on a hard floor than beside me.

I closed my eyes again, hoping to hide from his answers. If he was going to break it off with me, I'd rather not see it coming. Maybe I was a coward.

There was a slight noise before I felt the mattress lower as Mason sat down beside me. I instantly began rocking again, my body moving involuntarily, and it was seconds before I was encased in strong arms.

"I'm sorry about Jasmine. I'm sorry I couldn't save her. I'm sorry ...." I couldn't finish my sentence.

The calming, potent scent of wolf mixed with Mason hit me and I filled my lungs with it, memorizing it for future use. My heartbeat sought out his and slowed itself to match. My chest rose and fell in time with his. For the first time since I awoke, I felt some semblance of peace.

"Darcy, you think too much," Mason whispered, and he tightened his embrace. "It hurts me to hear you."

"It's true though," I murmured, "Why would you want me?"

"Because you're mine."

With that simple declaration, I fell apart.

Wave after wave of every emotion I lived through in the past twenty four hours washed over me, filling me up before erupting out in short, hard gasps. Drawing breath was near impossible as I panted through the pain and sobbed as my heart

73

broke all over again. As one cry finished, another began and everything faded away, leaving me drowning in grief. It was relentless—I couldn't escape it, forced to ride it out.

Slow, soothing strokes against my back were my lifeline, Mason's steady presence a reminder I wasn't alone, and I clutched onto him as my anchor. Gradually, my chest stopped tightening and my cries turned into muffled hiccups as I buried my face into him.

"Are you okay?" Mason asked softly, his hand leaving my back to run his fingers through my hair. His voice sounded thick with emotion, and a quick glance at his face confirmed my suspicions. I hadn't wept alone.

He'd also lost his sister, and I felt selfish for losing sight of it. He'd gone through the night alone, wanting to let me rest, choosing to see to my needs before his own. Love surged through me over this man, and I offered up a vow right then and there, I'd stand by him forever.

Pulling back slightly, I reached up and tenderly brushed away his tears with the pad of my thumb. Mason returned the favor, his focus never leaving my face. I'm not sure how I missed it before. Yes, there was a look of weariness and deep sadness, but there was also love blazing in his eyes. This was a man who adored me, who would wage war with the Devil himself, and he was all mine. My wolf howled in agreement.

You better believe I'm all yours. It's you and me forever, Darcy. No matter what.

He spoke again into my mind, and I tentatively reached out to answer him. *I love you, Mason. I'm so sorry.* I couldn't help let go of a sigh at being able to connect with him mentally. It troubled me that it hadn't worked earlier and before I could ask why, he interrupted me.

"There's plenty of time to talk, babe. We'll work on

it. Right now, I just want to make sure you're okay. You scared me last night and I hate feeling that way. I'm struggling with the death of Jasmine, but to think I almost lost you too ... I don't think I would survive that."

"Even a big bad wolf like you?" I offered a weak smile as I stroked his cheek, touched at the emotion he was showing me.

"Yes, even a big bad wolf like me. You're everything to me, Darcy. So I don't ever want to hear you think about leaving. Whatever happens, we face it together." There was a fierceness in his face now as he spoke, a determination that told me what he just shared was as good as law. Without thought, I leaned forward and brought my lips against his, moving them for a gentle, tender kiss.

"Thank you," I whispered, retreating slowly. A flash of hunger fired in his eyes before he pulled back, a look of concern returning to its place. Without warning, Mason lifted me into his arms, and with his back against the headboard, nestled me on his lap. I couldn't help but squeak at the sudden movement and blushed at how very un-wolf-like it was.

His slight chuckle resonated through my back as I got comfortable. Trust him to have heard it. Nothing escaped his notice when it came to me, and he brought his arms around my body, folding me into his own.

"Want to talk about it?" The question hung in the air and I didn't know how to answer. Everything inside me screamed to keep silent, to bury it deep, but the look of concern on his face told me he needed this just as much as I did.

I nodded and searched for a place to start. I wasn't looking forward to reliving it, but hopefully once it was out in the open between us we could heal together. Without any more thought, I opened my mouth and the words poured out. They came slowly at first, and then rapidly. The purging felt good.

Mason sat quietly, focused on letting me set the pace, but there was no denying the inner turmoil he was going through. As he listened about the threat to me and his sister, and the struggle she went through, electricity churned in the air. His wolf was right at the surface, chomping and snarling, wanting to be released. It showed the amazing strength and control he had, because a lesser wolf would've changed under the incredible pressure.

Even with his fury tightly reined, Mason emitted low growls. When I retold the moment where Jasmine was shot, he leaned his head back and let out the most haunted, terrifying cry I'd ever heard. It was full of grief, maddening in its intensity. His arms became like iron rods around me and I knew all his protective instincts had kicked in. Had I not already taken care of Gary, Mason would've left right at that moment, and not stopped until he destroyed the monster who dared to steal from him.

I turned my body to sit across his lap so I could reach up to his face. With my fingers, I traced the outline of his cheek. Tenderly, I brought his gaze to mine and it was just as I suspected—his eyes were wolf-like, more evidence of his battle to keep his beast caged. I pulled him closer and kissed his eyelids, resting my forehead against his when I was finished.

We sat quietly, lost in the moment, clinging to one another. When I felt the change in the air and Mason relax, I looked back and related the rest of the tale. I told how my wolf had taken charge, hunting the threat down like prey and relishing in the kill. I shared everything, hoping this would bring him a sense of justice. From the look of feral triumph he gave me, I hoped it would be enough.

I stared at him for the longest time, trying to judge what he'd do. I knew he was in turmoil, I could see it in his body language and in the way he tightly held me. I caught my breath—waiting. He answered me moments later. One minute I was sitting in his lap, and next I was airborne.

Mason's strength always amazed me. Flipping me over so I was lying on my back, he hovered above me. I opened my mouth to ask what he was doing, but a soft growl and focused look stopped me in my tracks.

Without another word spoken, he set about inspecting every part of my body. He was methodical in his approach, lifting and studying, looking for anything that showed signs of abuse. Every inch met his gaze, and he released small grunts of satisfaction before moving on to the next. I lay there and let him, knowing he wouldn't simply take my word for it, he needed to see for himself.

Once he was finished, he started again, but this time his touches were different. Gone was the restlessness. Mason was now moving about like a man wanting to memorize and reclaim what was his. You are mine, he repeated and he lowered his face to smell my skin. Licking me in slow circles, he feathered me with soft kisses. I was helpless to fight the pull of passion stirring between us.

There was something erotic about the way he moved over me, his heated build pressed hard against mine. I couldn't help the way my body reacted as I arched into his touch and sighed with deep contentment. When Mason found a certain sensitive spot, one he loved to tease me with, I decided I'd had enough and reached for him.

One moment my hands were touching him and the next they were pinned to the bed while he looked down at me wickedly. "Patience, Darcy. I'm not finished. There's one more place I haven't savored."

I held my breath, desire coursing through me and almost lost my mind as he nestled into my neck, nipping and sucking at the tender flesh. It was definitely a weakness of mine, the feel of his teeth and lips, the brushing of heated breath. I squirmed against him, trying to break from his restraining grip. All it did was add fuel to the fire already building between us.

"Mason, you're killing me here. Please." I wasn't beneath begging for him to kiss me.

He chuckled, a deep, throaty laugh that weakened me further. "You scared me. I told you not to go out alone and I was right. All your sass," he said, biting at my neck, the slight sting causing a moan to escape from my mouth. "Your assurances everything would be okay." He swirled his tongue slowly, bringing goose bumps to my flesh. "I want you to say it—I was right and you were wrong." Having finished in that spot, he moved on to the next. "Admit it."

I shook my head, but not out of stubbornness. Heck, I was ready to declare to the world I was wrong, but I knew Mason. He had some wicked plan brewing that involved delicious punishment and I was definitely not going to rob him of his moment.

He tightened his grip on my wrists, and prodded my ear with his nose. "Say it, Darcy, or I'll make you scream it."

I realized while I was focused on the seductive magic he was creating with his mouth, I hadn't noticed he removed one of his hands, holding me with just one while his free hand roamed over my body. The sudden awareness of it sent wave after wave of heat through me, as his touch left a blazing trail, scorching my insides.

I looked into his eyes, determined to give him a look which said, "Bring it," but instead I melted under the fierce intensity staring back at me. He was serious. He'd make me scream and no doubt from incredible pleasure.

I felt my lips curl as I cooed suggestively back at him, "What are you waiting for?"

Mason needed no more convincing. His lips came crushing down on mine, robbing me of breath and causing my mouth to open as I gasped for air. Seizing the opportunity, he wasted no time slipping in, and I felt myself explode under the sensation of his tongue dancing with mine. If there was one thing he did well, it was kissing and this was nothing short of magnificent.

I gave myself over, allowing him to lead, holding nothing back. It was pure emotion and chemistry between us, the magic of who we were to each other left tingling in the air. We were to be mated, bound together through centuries of tradition, but it was way more than that. Mason and I had a soul deep connection that over time would grow stronger and impenetrable. I loved this man, and I poured it all into our kiss.

I jumped a little as I felt his hand slide under my shirt and rest on my stomach, his fingers stroking my skin. I marveled at how responsive I was to his caress, how a single touch held the power to undo me, leaving me almost without reason. I yearned for him, craved his attentions and the intensity of my desire burned me to the core. This moment felt so right. He felt so right, and I wasn't the only one short of breath when we finally pulled apart.

"You were right," I whispered. Realizing my

hands had been released, I reached up and traced Mason's lips, still moist from our kiss. "I promise I'll always listen to you in the future."

He nipped at my finger, sucking it slightly into his mouth before he let out a soft laugh. "No you won't, Darcy. You'll fight me tooth and nail over the things important to you but it's okay. We'll work through my need to keep you safe and your ability to drive me insane." He went to lean back in, but he paused as I raised my hands up to his lips.

"We shouldn't be doing this, Mason. We can't act as if nothing has happened or changed. You've lost your sister, and I know you're worried about me, but you need to be cared for as well." I brushed my fingers lightly across his jawline, the softness of his stubble creating slight friction. "This isn't just about me."

Catching my hand, he tenderly kissed my palm. "I know we need to talk more about Jasmine, and we'll grieve for our loss together, but when I think about how close I came to losing both of you ... I need to be able to touch you right now. I need to know you are safe, and alive. You scared me, and hearing you talk of leaving is unacceptable. There will be time for everything, Darcy. Trust me to know this is what I feel we both need."

The look in his eyes spoke volumes. It asked that I give in to his sincerity, and stop resisting. Feathering his hair with my hand, brushing it from his brow, I nodded. He was telling me by helping me, he was also helping himself.

We stared at each other for a moment and I could feel the strength of our connection between us. I raised my head to his, but was interrupted by the hesitant knocking at the door. I flopped back onto the bed. There's only one reason someone would willingly disturb the Alpha when he was alone with his future mate—Pack business.

I waited for Mason to answer, but he seemed more focused on me, watching me intently. He lifted his finger to his mouth to shush me and smiled. Pressing his lips against mine, it was obvious he was ready to continue what we were doing before.

I giggled. He had lost his sense of seriousness and was in a playful mood. Unfortunately, whoever was on the other side of door couldn't see it as they increased the forcefulness of their knock, determined to have someone answer.

"Mason?" A cautious voice came from the hallway.

The knocking intensified and turning toward the sound, Mason let out a loud growl, instantly silencing the noise. A second later I could hear the shuffling of footsteps as the pack member escaped. No one ignored the Alpha.

"So where were we?" He smiled, returning his focus to me. His eyes shone and I could see his wolf at the surface. It took a few seconds before they returned back to normal.

"You don't think you should've answered that? It was important enough for them to face the wrath of their Alpha."

"It can wait. This won't." He leaned in again, kissing me until I could no longer remember my name.

"My, you really are a big, bad wolf." I sighed when we finally pulled apart. My body felt completely languid, relaxed under his masterful touch and attention.

"Of course, nothing but the best for you, baby," Mason punctuated his statement with another quick kiss. I loved seeing this side of him—the fierce and protective warrior, the determined and passionate lover.

I couldn't help myself as I reached out to feel his face again. I caressed his cheek, running my fingers through his hair, knowing I wore a goofy smile as I did.

"So, is this where I say, "Oh, what big eyes you have," Mr. Big, Bad Wolf?"

Mischief lit his stare and a devious smirk covered his lips. "Only if you want to hear, "All the better to see you with, my dear." He made a point to sweep a knowing look over me before returning back to my gaze.

"I would then feel compelled to add, "Oh, what big ears you have."

"All the better to hear you with, Darcy." Mason played along, lowering his voice to a seductive whisper.

I brushed my finger over his bottom lip, eliciting a quick snap of his teeth. "Oh, what big teeth you have." It came out breathless with anticipation, and I felt my body tense.

He paused, cocking his head to the side. He knew the next line, what he was meant to say, but nothing came. Hunger bore into me, desire coming off him in waves. I waited for him to finish—to ravish me. Instead, with a look I couldn't quite decipher, he pulled back and rose to his feet.

What the heck is he doing?

Confused, I watched Mason look around the room. With a slight nod, he finally moved, scooping me up in his arms before plastering me against the closest wall.

"All the better to eat you with, my dear, and this looks like the ideal place for a sample." With his left hand placed firmly by my head and his right secured around my waist, he bent slightly and nibbled at my mouth. Gentle brushes of his lips teased me back and forth and left me wanting more.

"Hmmm, this won't do at all." I felt myself being hoisted up, my legs wrapping easily around his waist.

With my arms around his neck, I was pressed snuggly against him, my body beginning to melt into his.

Mason tugged at my hair, giving him better access to my mouth and neck. He leaned down, burying his face below my ear and took in a deep, long breath. "Yes, this is much better."

His kiss came hard and fast, impressively dominating and full of animalistic desire. There was no holding back as he completed his need to reclaim and reassert his stance as my intended mate. It was a kiss that overshadowed any we previously shared and boldly declared a warning to anyone foolish enough to touch me again.

I barely heard the sound of the door abruptly open and the muffled laugh and cough of whoever entered.

"Well, what do we have here? No wonder you're not answering, My Esteemed Liege. Looks like you may have more pressing matters to undress ... I mean address."

Mason snarled, but it didn't deter the intruder for letting out a hearty chuckle. "By all means, Your Most Elevated Highness, continue. I'll just sit over on the chair and wait, shall I?"

"You are aware pissing me off could warrant a death penalty? I've killed for far less than this," Mason finally answered. There was a subtle hint of softness to his voice, a sign of friendly banter. Sometimes his bark was worse than his bite.

"Whatever. Who else would you get to guard your sorry butt then if you got rid of me? Seriously, Your Royal Eminence, take your time. Finish what you were doing, I appreciate a good show."

A quick breeze and a loud crash told me Mason had retaliated to the goading by throwing a lamp at

Daniel, his best friend and second-in-command.

"Hey, watch the furniture. I liked that!" I slapped at him, trying to lower my legs to the floor. I instantly met with resistance as Mason grabbed my legs and held them in place.

"I'll buy you a new one and don't move. He won't be staying, will you?" He directed the question back at the guy now reclined lazily on my armchair. The piles of clothes I had on it moments ago were now dumped on the floor in a careless heap.

I peered around Mason's body and grinned at Daniel. "Hey."

A look of concern and compassion replaced the previous cockiness. "Hey, sweetheart. You doing okay? You sure did scare us." That seemed to be the general consensus and I nodded, indicating I was fine.

"Good. I don't ever want to arrive on a scene and see that again, do you hear me? No more going off by yourself." Daniel noted the look Mason gave him and chuckled again, "Looks like Our Most Excellent and Noble One has already covered that and moved onto the punishing phase."

"Is there a reason why you're still here?" Impatience was beginning to creep into Mason's voice. I wasn't helping matters either as I begun to nudge my lips against his neck, placing soft kisses.

"There is, my most Beloved Benefactor."

I couldn't help it. Laughter exploded out of my mouth and I threw my head back in mirth.

"What the heck is going on? Liege? Beloved Benefactor? Royal Eminence? Since when do people address you like that, Mason? Or should I say Most Magnificent Master?"

Mason dragged me away from resting on the wall quick enough to swat my behind with his hand. "Enough! Don't encourage him, Darcy. Daniel has gotten it into his head I'm not being paid enough respect as the Alpha and is trying to instill in the younger pack members the importance of titles. I can't turn around without someone bowing or spouting off some crazy name. Nothing I've done can convince them it's not necessary. It's driving me insane." He puffed out a quick breath in frustration.

"Which is why I will continue," Daniel interrupted, ducking as another piece of my furniture went flying. Mason rolled his eyes and grinned before turning back to look at his friend.

I lowered myself to the ground, Mason letting me this time, and I fully joined the conversation. "What's going on?"

Daniel gave a brief glance at his Alpha and I saw a slight nod returned.

"Devlin called and asked after Darcy and Jasmine. I filled him in with what happened and the mention of vampire blood raised a lot of questions. He's on his way over with condolences from Zane and to see what needs to be done. He sounded furious."

I saw Mason take in the information and knew he had to be thinking about what it all meant. Devlin was one of the Enforcers set up by the vampire leader, Zane, to investigate and eliminate any threats to the supernatural community. The thought of humans having access to such potent blood had to be disturbing.

"How long before he gets here?"

"Well, when we first tried to tell you, you had an hour." Daniel checked his watch. "Now you have about twenty minutes." He looked back expectantly at Mason, waiting for orders. All joking was pushed aside as business was approaching.

"Okay, when he arrives, show him into my

office and we'll meet you there." I knew Mason felt the flash of fear that spun out of control inside me. I didn't want to repeat last night's events, in any way. He grabbed hold of my hand and squeezed it.

"Give us a moment to prepare," he ordered.

Daniel pulled himself out of the chair and started to make his way to the door. Before he left, he stopped in front of me, bowing his head slightly in respect.

"I'm glad you're okay, Darcy. I'm sorry about Jasmine."

Tears began to well in my eyes again, and a knot formed in my throat. I had no other choice but to reply with a nod of my own.

With the door closed and Mason and I finally alone again, he pulled me back into his arms as more tears started to fall. He moved his hand in slow, comforting strokes against my back.

"Will you be able to come to the meeting? Heaven knows, I don't want to cause you any more distress but it's important Devlin hears it all from you."

"I'll be fine. It needs to be done. I'm just so sorry." Sobs broke out and the feelings of contentment Mason inspired in me earlier were replaced with ones of sorrow and guilt.

I felt my chin being tilted up as he sought my gaze. "Hey, I thought we dealt with this? No guilt, remember. We'll get through this together." I couldn't answer for crying.

I could almost sense the moment when he came to some decision. "You know what? More important business has just come up. Devlin can wait. Come on."

Releasing me from his embrace, Mason began pulling me toward the door. He paused a second, stopping, and moved to the window. Opening it, he extended his hand out in invitation.

"What about ...?"

"No questions, Darcy. Just come."

I placed my hand in his and together we escaped through the pane. Moving with stealth, Mason led me into the neighboring woods that encompassed the borders of his property. This was pack land, handed down from generation to generation and it was lush with all the different shades of green and browns.

The house was set on a huge estate, the grounds designed specifically to offer protection from prying eyes. But the acres of woodlands were my favorite. It was filled with wildlife that made each full moon exciting because it offered a variety of prey to hunt.

Barely a few yards into the trees, he turned and begun undressing, signaling for me to do the same. "Unless you'd like me to do it for you?" he asked, cocking one of his eyebrows as a challenge.

The thought of changing and going for a run infused me with an infectious energy, and I grinned. I frantically began pulling at my clothes, lifting my shirt over my head and stepping out of my jeans. With a wink and a kiss, I began the process.

"Catch me if you can."

The last thing I heard was the promise, Believe me, I will.

Chapter Six

I didn't wait for Mason to finish before I took off running, relishing the instant sense of freedom. Happiness blazed through me as I darted in and out amongst the trees, my sleek wolf body giving me an agility I lacked when in my human form.

My wolf instantly came to the forefront, eager to assert control. Sniffing the air, she scanned for danger and when she was confident all was well, only then did she settle back down. I learned early on, the only time she would take over and push me into the background was if she determined the situation too dangerous. Last night was a classic example. I realized now I never had a chance in hell of staying in the driver's seat once I changed. With no prevailing threat, I was able to still be me in wolf form, and I yipped with excitement.

I increased my speed, paws hitting the ground at a furious pace as I fought to race the wind itself. The constant stream of cool air blowing through my fur felt invigorating, and I bayed with delight along with my wolf as we let go to nature.

My ears flickered as my eyes scanned the surrounding area, expecting to hear the approach of Mason, but I couldn't pick up anything other than the noises of nearby wildlife. Worry struck and I sent out my senses to see if I could feel anything.

Nothing yet. Shaking off my concern, I focused

back on the task at hand—running as if chased by the Devil.

Foliage crumpled under my stride as I leapt over fallen trees and muddied patches of ground. Raising my nose to the air, I was assaulted with the aroma of freshly churned soil and the hint of a previous rain. I took the smells deep into my lungs, savoring the way they tasted on my tongue and howled with enthusiasm. This was definitely one of the best parts of being a werewolf—experiencing the world on the most basic of levels. No human cares or distractions. No judgment—just me, my wolf, and our surroundings. Mason was right to have us go on a run. Nothing could help me refocus more.

Where is he? I tried to reach for him through our connection and immediately felt a sense of nothing. Was he blocking me?

A flash of black from the corner of my eye was all the warning I had before I was attacked. My fur rose into hackles and I started to prepare to defend myself. A familiar scent bombarded me and I growled in triumph.

So he wanted to play?

I wiggled out from under him. Mason, having the element of surprise, had pinned me to the ground with his strong paws.

Swiping at his nose, I settled back into a crouch, shaking my tail in invitation. I barked out the equivalent of a taunt and sent the mental image of me standing over him, while he shook in submission.

His good humored laughter was my reply and he began to stalk me, pacing in circles, watching carefully. All the while, I returned the best bored look I could muster. Testing to see if he could get the upper hand, he attempted a few lunges, but I saw them coming and quickly leapt out of his reach.

Tired of the dance we were doing, I took the attack

to him, springing forward hard and fast, bowling him over in a mess of fur and paws. I nipped at his neck and before he could get himself situated, took off again into the trees. Mason's howl told me the game was on.

We played, enjoying one another away from the responsibility of our lives. With all the energy we were burning, frolicking quickly gave way to hunger, and I suddenly became aware we were surrounded by wildlife.

Wait here.

He didn't give me a chance to respond before he bounded off into the shrubbery, leaving me alone to settle into a spot to wait for his return.

I must've dozed off because the next thing I knew I heard a thump as something small was tossed at my feet. Opening a lazy eye, I noticed Mason crouched in front of me, a small rabbit lying by my paws. He crawled forward and with his nose, nudged the food closer to me.

I took a bite of the rabbit, my teeth tearing through fur and flesh. Normally, as a human, this would make me cringe, but as a wolf, it was as natural as breathing.

Thank you, I shared with him. Thanks for taking care of me.

Always, he replied. Now eat.

I tried rolling some of what was left back toward him, suggesting we share, but with a wolfy grin, Mason trotted over to a tree and brought out his own kill. We sat in silence as we began to dig in. Eating with relish, my stomach was soon full and content, and I moved closer to Mason, absorbing the heat of his body into mine.

I slowly began the process of licking him, making sure he was cleaned after a messy meal and then laid back as he returned the favor. There was a soothing sense of "rightness" between us and I knew this was how it would always be. I felt cherished, loved and protected.

Once we were finished, I stood up and shook out my fur, stretching out my limbs from sitting down such a long time. Mason began to pull away and once again issued a command.

Come.

We broke out into a run. Careful to follow his lead, I took every chance I could to bump my body against him as we kept a steady pace. I was curious to see where he was taking me because the house was back in the opposite direction.

I came to a screeching halt as we broke free of the trees. Before us was one of the most breathtaking scenes I'd ever seen. How I'd never known this place existed was beyond me. I started the Change and stepped forward on human feet. Everywhere my eyes looked, I saw perfection and a small slice of heaven. Mason came up from behind and wrapped his arms around me.

"I've been waiting for the right time to bring you here. I've been coming here for the last couple of months since I discovered it. I wanted to share it with you." He rested his chin on my shoulder as I stood there, trying to describe what I was seeing.

Mason had brought me to a waterfall. Not as large as some I'd seen, but the cascading water fell steadily into a pool that looked deep enough to swim in. The sound of the water crashing on the rocks below resonated in me and I could feel a sense of enveloping peace. The smells of wet, fresh vegetation surrounded us and the air was the perfect temperature for a quick dip.

He must've known where my thoughts were leading

because he lifted me up and carried me to the edge of the pool, gently placing me on the rocks so my feet could dangle in the refreshing liquid. Confidently, he strode into the depths, not flinching as the coolness battled with the heat of his body and he stood in between my legs.

"What about Devlin? He's not going to like being made to wait." I asked, knowing there was more important matters to take care of. I appreciated the chance to run, having needed it more than I realized, but I couldn't let my needs distract Mason from his responsibilities.

"Right now Darcy, I don't want you worrying about it. Devlin can wait. All you need do is relax and leave everything else up to me. Just accept I know what we need right now."

I nodded, amazed at the incredible strength of the love I saw on his face.

Yep, cherished.

There was no denying it. I closed my eyes and waited for Mason to begin.

I heard trickling as he lifted my left foot out of the water, using his hands to massage out the tension in my muscles. He dripped the cool fluid over my toes, drawing a wet line up my ankle and over my shin. He followed it with soft kisses, before returning my foot to the water and starting on the right.

His touch felt magical, almost reverent as he began to slowly caress each part of me, first with slow, erotic circles and then showering it with droplets. I peeked through my eyelashes as he worked his way up past my knees, concentrating on my thighs, each movement causing my breath to hitch. I couldn't help but realize the seriousness and importance of the moment.

Quietly, he took hold of my hips and lifted me into his arms, backing up into the water before submerging my body completely under. I shuddered at the sensation, not just because I found myself fully immersed, but also from the smolder I saw in Mason's eyes. There was complete focus.

Holding me close enough to offer security, he tipped me back and worked his hands through my hair, separating the strands as they floated on the surface.

I closed my eyes again, showing my trust in him. I felt his hand hold me firmly at the base of my back, keeping me safely afloat. Moments later I felt a stream of water on my exposed chest and stomach. Mason's hand followed, trailing a lazy path over my skin as he chased the droplets with his fingers.

Beautiful, his thoughts came through loud and clear. Mine.

His hands continued their careful ministrations and it struck me what he was doing, the symbolism humbling me. Mason had done everything short of removing the horrible memories of last night. He didn't hold that power, but he could do the next best thing in his mind—he could wash them away. The act took on a whole new perspective and brought fresh tears to my eyes.

How did I ever win this man's heart and loyalty? I felt myself pulled against Mason's body, completely relaxed and wet. My skin felt slippery against his, and it was obvious he was just as aroused as I was.

I brushed a strand of hair away from his eyes, hoping I could show him how much this meant to me. "You're perfect," I whispered before he kissed me.

His gentleness almost undid me. Gone was the fiery passion of earlier when it seemed he couldn't get enough of me. This was a savoring kiss, one that said he had all the time in the world to explore my mouth. It told me he considered me the most precious thing in the world and he never wanted to let me go.

He softly nipped before sucking slowly on my bottom lip. His tongue stroked with an unhurried, steady pace as he finally entered my mouth. I couldn't help the purr I created or the groan of satisfaction I heard from Mason. For the length of our kiss it was just the two of us, and I soaked it up.

I realized we'd returned to the shore when my back hit the side of the rocks. He lifted me up, setting me onto the rough surface and my body thrilled at the thought of what might come next. I enjoyed the scene as he pulled himself out of the water, standing over me.

Werewolves naturally have fit physiques—all leanness and well-toned muscle. But there was something about Mason, the way he carried himself that was graceful yet masculine all at the same time. Every inch of his body was glorious, a combination of hardness and sculpted contours. I never got tired of watching him move or the way he had a trail of hair that went from his sternum and over his abdomen. I wanted to stroke him, lick him, and feel all that power under my fingertips.

"We'll have plenty of time for that, Darcy." He chuckled, finding the sudden pout on my lips amusing. "First, let's talk."

"Talk? Now you want to talk?" Standing up, I looked over at him with my hands on my hips. By the flare in his eyes as he looked over my naked body, I didn't think he would need much convincing.

Without a word, he moved toward a nearby tree and pulled out something from behind it. I raised my eyebrows and was surprised to see him holding a blanket.

"I brought it here last time and forgot to take it back with me. Just as well, I need you to cover up so I can protect you." He held it open and I unwillingly stepped into it. The warmth and softness of the material felt good against my skin and I found myself cocooned.

"Protect me from what? We're alone."

He took a seat against the trunk of a tree that shadowed over the pool. Nestling me on his lap, he answered. "From me, the big bad wolf, remember? Looking the way you did, you were too tempting and it was all I could do not to nibble on you." He kissed the top of my head. "Besides, it's time we air out your thoughts."

My thoughts. I couldn't help the shiver that erupted through me. I didn't want to think anymore. I wanted Mason and my body demanded I take what I needed.

I could've strangled him as he laughed and I looked at him accusingly.

"You get me all hot and bothered—you show me how much you love me, and now you want to chat?" I tried my best to protest but failed miserably. I just wasn't that kind of girl.

He reached for a strand of my hair and twirled it around his fingers. He looked thoughtful, and I resigned myself to the moment. There was no point in avoiding it, the sooner we could talk the better, and I had a few questions of my own to ask.

"So where do you want to start?" I asked tentatively.

His fingers stopped and trailed down the side of my cheek, his gaze full of seriousness.

"Would you have really left me?" he whispered, his hurt lying just beneath the surface. "I heard your thoughts earlier when you first woke up. Would it have been that easy?"

"It would've killed me, but in that moment, it

seemed like the only thing to do." I answered just as softly. "I love you so much, but I can't help but feel like I've failed you. How could I expect you to forgive me? I had a responsibility to Jasmine and instead of doing what was necessary, I hesitated. All I can see in my mind is what would've happened if I'd changed and eliminated the threat. All I can think is why am I so adamant about being human when I'm a werewolf? What happened was inexcusable and I've brought shame to myself, and ultimately to you. Do you really want a mate who everyone thinks is a coward?" The last sentence blasted out and the question hung in the air. I pushed myself away from Mason and began to pace back and forth in front of him.

"You know, as your mate, every single wolf who feels they have something to prove will throw down a challenge. If I can't protect one of our own from a human," I spat the name out as if it was poison, "How the hell am I supposed to protect them from greater threats? You need strength by your side, not weakness. Not me." It stunned me how passionately I felt about this. It didn't mean I was ready to pack my bags and leave, I understood where my place was and where I wanted to be, but this had to be spoken otherwise it would fester forever. I needed Mason to hear how strongly this affected me, how deeply it had shaken my foundation. I just prayed I could come back from it.

"When have you ever been asked to be strong, Darcy?" He moved to stand and comfort me. I thrust out my hand to stop him, growling a warning that it wasn't the time. I didn't need comforting. I needed to purge.

"It's what's expected!" I screamed, tears finally falling down my cheeks. "As your mate, I will always hold the standard and expectation to be infallible. Mistakes can't happen. Not in the Alpha and the woman he chooses to bond with. I thought I was made of stronger stuff, I really did. " I felt his gaze follow me as I reached my hand up to the tree and plucked off a leaf. I was silent for a moment, trying to regain my composure. My fingers worked shakily at shredding the small foliage, tiny pieces of it fluttering to the floor before I dropped the stem to the ground. I went to pull another but thought better of it. The tree hadn't done anything to warrant my destroying part of it. I scowled and resumed pacing.

"I love you so much it hurts. I can't imagine not having you in my life, waking up each morning knowing I'm blessed enough to be mated to a man who is everything I could ever hope for. I love knowing you will forever be the first and last thing I see each day, but I'll not be your downfall. I couldn't bear it—so yes, I would've left, but don't ever believe it would've been easy."

I threw myself down beside him and pulled my knees into my chest to hug them. I shook so hard I was surprised I didn't rattle myself to pieces. Strong emotion coursed through me, spiking my adrenaline levels so hard it was a wonder I hadn't changed. I felt beneath the surface for my wolf and for once she was quiet. She wasn't there howling or demanding freedom. She also sensed it wasn't just important for me to get this out, but was also crucial to her future. A werewolf divided within itself was dangerous. I felt her brush up against my skin in support and dragged in a deep breath, hoping it would settle me. I was angry—at myself, at Gary, and everyone, including Mason.

"Why?" I looked at him pleadingly, before banging my fist against his shoulder. "Why didn't you come?" I fell apart and this time didn't resist when he pulled me into his arms again. I felt his hand stroke the back of my head and the slight shush sound he made as he struggled to soothe me.

"I know it was my fault. I should've listened to you when you said it wasn't safe. There was nothing wrong in taking extra protection. I was wrong to fight and now Jasmine is gone, but you should've come." I couldn't hold back any longer and I felt his arms tighten as the electricity in the air began to crackle.

Even as I heard myself blame him for not being there, I knew it wasn't right. There was no way Mason could've known because my ability to use our connection was sketchy at best.

It was one of those things where you tell yourself, "I know I need to work on this, but hey, everything is safe so there's no rush." We're counseled to prepare for every situation, for peace and war, but I had been arrogant. I'd constantly put it off, and when I met Mason I declared since I was to be the Alpha's mate, didn't that mean I could do it at will? My pride had vicious consequences.

I felt him take in a breath as he prepared to speak, but I wasn't finished, and even as the words flew out, I cringed. "You said you would protect me. You promised and where were you?"

I sobbed so hard my chest felt like it was on fire, and I struggled to regain my breath. Everything hurt—my body, my heart and I knew I wasn't the only one.

"Will you let me speak now, Darcy?" Mason queried.

I nodded against his chest, and absently used my hand to wipe away the collection of tears. His skin was hot to the touch, and I could feel his blood thrumming beneath the surface. He was tightly leashed and I braced myself for the outpouring of anger I knew had to be coming. How could he not after my attack?

It was unfair to pour my anger and blame him because I felt guilty over my inadequacies. I knew it the moment I'd opened my mouth, but I hadn't been able to pull myself back from spewing forth the words.

"If I could, I would rip Gary limb from damn limb— slowly, painfully, for him placing these doubts in your mind." Mason spat through clenched teeth. "The fact you sit here, twisted in knots, questioning the value you hold—to not just me, but the pack, makes me wish a thousand painful deaths on the traitor."

I was incredulous and whipped my head up suddenly, desperate to catch his meaning. Eyes blazing with an anger that could have leveled a city met mine, but it wasn't directed at me. Mason had been able to see to the heart of the matter and place the blame firmly at the feet of the true villain.

"How can you not be furious at me?"

"Is that what you're wanting, Darcy? Will it help if I rant and rail at you, shredding what little confidence you have left? Really?" He looked searchingly into my eyes, the hard stare of an Alpha. "I know you feel you need to claim this burden and I can understand why. But not once have I blamed you for anything that has happened. If anything, the guilt would fall on my shoulders as Alpha because I ignored my instinct to go with you or at the very least send someone with you."

Pain lanced my heart as I heard him assume the responsibility. To hear him accuse himself was too much. I began to speak, but he gently placed his finger over my lips to silence me. For a brief moment, he traced their outline and I savored the touch.

"My turn, remember?" He continued, I blushed, settling into him, and pulling his arms back around me.

The feeling of security was instant, and I clung to it.

"But, Darcy, despite the "what if's," despite any feelings of fault I may want to assign, the fact of the matter is the ultimate responsibility lies with Gary. We trusted him and thought he was a friend. Last night was about his actions. You and Jasmine unfortunately got caught in the cross fire. Regardless of what you think, you handled it fine. There was no right and wrong. You saw a threat and you acted."

"Like a coward, though."

"No, as the strong, compassionate woman I know and love. You say you have to be this strong and infallible leader and mate. Never has that been an expectation, and I don't know why you would think that. All I ask—all I will ever ask is that you be yourself. We're a team and we both bring traits to this relationship that will strengthen us and help us lead the Pack together. I count on the compassion you showed last night. On your ability to think first and seeing if there is a more peaceful solution before rushing into a situation. Yes, you saw a threat to both you and Jasmine, but you also saw a friend and before you acted as judge and executioner, you tried to resolve it. That shows the marks of an honorable leader. Don't ever doubt it and don't bury it under whatever you think you should be. You are perfect in my eyes, and I wouldn't have you any other way. Understand?"

If I could've spoken, I would've told him just how much his words had reached in and soothed me. I felt the burden I'd been carrying ease slightly, and a lightness which hadn't been there since this whole fiasco had started.

"Whenever you begin to doubt your worth, Darcy, come to me. I'll show and keep showing you until it's so entrenched in that beautiful, stubborn head of yours, you'll start seeing yourself as I see you."

Images and memories began to form in my mind as Mason was true to his word, showing me what he saw and felt as he watched me each day. He was so observant, catching every subtle change in my facial expressions and body language. He had been studying me and it now made sense why he could read me so well. He was the diligent student and I was his favorite subject.

His emotions flowed over my skin and settled, filling me with a sense of wonder at being loved so completely. There were flashes of brief frustration, and as I watched the images they were attached to, they were times I was being pig headed—adamant in doing things my own way. But they were quickly replaced with feelings of pride and satisfaction in loving a woman who was confident to speak her mind and knew how to fight for what she believed in. He even found it humorous I had no problem going toe-to-toe with him. No one ever questioned him and he actually looked forward to our mini battles.

I couldn't witness his feelings or memories and deny he was incredibly happy as well as deeply in love with me. After everything, he was still one hundred percent commitment and devoted. Before I could think more on it, his voice interrupted the silence.

"This is what I want you to see." And he recalled the moment we met.

Chapter Seven

I remembered the day. We'd definitely met under strange circumstances, but we joked about it later. Fate doesn't care how she brings two people together, as long as she does. After a night of dreaming about Mason—a vision that felt so incredibly real, I'd woken to a phone call from my mother.

She was unbending in her belief she could hear my biological clock ticking away into oblivion. I tried, desperately, to assure her there was plenty of time for mates and babies, but she was determined to have me bonded and shipped off as soon as I hit my twenties. I couldn't remember how many eligible werewolves she paraded in front of me over the years, each one "the one." As I turned every one of them down, I'd leave my poor mother an exasperated mess. She just didn't get it. I was waiting for something ... that spark, the moment where my stomach tipped as butterflies stirred. I wanted passion and the sense of certainty knowing I'd met my soul mate.

I'll never forget the day I tried explaining that to her. It resulted in an angry tirade about how I was breaking her heart and being an ungrateful whelp. The love I was wanting wasn't important, she claimed, all I needed was a strong werewolf mate who could provide and protect me. She almost choked on her tongue when I defiantly stood there, hands on hips and declared I didn't even know if I'd marry a werewolf. I didn't want to be controlled and dominated over. Her face turned a mottled shade of red before she stormed out of my house, muttering about how she didn't know who I was. The next day I came home to all my beloved romance novels shredded and unceremoniously dumped into trash bags. A note was left on my dining room table.

Darcy, I blame the nonsense you read in these books for your insane idea of marriage. It's time you realize there are no heroes to sweep you off your feet. Pick a mate and settle. It's time.

Settle. Out of everything she'd said on the page, that word jumped out like it was written on a neon sign. It was one thing I'd never do. I'd rather die old and alone than ever settle for something less. It also made me sad wondering if that's what she had done with my father.

We never did talk about the note and her destroying my books. We continued as we normally did—her sending me candidates and me tolerating her. I found a better place to put my books, and life carried on.

The day she called, she was excited about a man she'd met who she thought would be perfect for me.

"It's like he stepped out of one of those books you love so much," she chattered over the phone. "Surely you won't find fault with him as well. Just wait until you meet him." She continued to prattle on and I tuned her out.

I couldn't help but groan. One thing I loathed was blind dates because they were just so painfully awkward. There was the overwhelming need to fill every moment with something so we wouldn't spend the entire date in unbearable silence. Trying to think of a way to break it to the guy gently when it was obvious to me, it just wouldn't work.

I was already beginning to think of how I could

wheedle my way out of this meeting when the doorbell rang.

"Tell me you didn't, Mother," I interrupted. I had no doubt she knew what I was talking about. The woman had the ears of a hawk and would undoubtedly have heard the chimes.

"Just do this for me. I want grand babies, Darcy. Wear something pretty with your hair up. Men like that." I swear she was oblivious to how uncomfortable these meetings made me.

"Can you at least tell me what his name is?" I asked before I went to my doom.

"His name is Mason. Mason O'Connor. Be nice to him or so help me I'll ...." I cut her off mid rant as I quickly said goodbye and hung up. I'd heard her threats so many times I could rehearse them verbatim in my sleep.

The door chime rang again.

"Let's go see who the lucky contestant is," I grumbled under my breath. I swung the door open and was floored by the battering of emotions that hit me with such a force I staggered. I would've fallen if Mason hadn't reached out and grabbed hold of my arm.

"Already falling for me?" He chuckled, his eyes never leaving my face, his stare devouring.

Any other time I would've felt uncomfortable being under such intense scrutiny, but the look of hunger and triumph made my skin tingle and my breath hitched.

It was him. Don't ask me how or why, I wasn't a big believer in Fate, but standing before me, in all his glory was the guy from my dream. My wolf howled as she also recognized what it meant. Ours, she bayed over and over, stirring my insides into a frenzy.

Every wolf knows what this feeling means and it took everything I could not to launch myself at him as my wolf struggled to take control of the situation. We had met our mate and she was ready to claim him right there and then, ritual be damned.

I caught myself in time and I must have looked like I was having a fit as my body contorted before I stumbled again, and this time fell. So much for looking graceful.

Are you done reminiscing, Darcy? Are you ready to see what I saw that day? Mason interrupted, breaking my thoughts.

I nodded slightly and refocused back on the memory. This time it looked different as I saw my old front door.

I could feel the nervousness rippling under his skin as he bounced on his toes, waiting for me to answer the door. He wasn't sure what to expect and was hoping this wasn't another, "come-meet-my-beautiful-daughter, she's-perfect-for-you," situations. He stood there, thinking over all the things he could be doing, like pack business that demanded his attention. Instead, he was going on a blind date.

How the heck did I allow myself to get talked into this?

Mrs. Matthews was a tough woman to say no to, not to mention one that seemed hell bent to marry her daughter off. She'd been relentless and seemed to have a counter offer for every excuse he'd given her. For his own sanity, he'd agreed to meet her daughter, Darcy, and silently prayed they'd at least be able to talk.

He rubbed his face, letting out a deep breath. A feeling of frustration washed through him as he thought about the pressure he was receiving from everyone to hurry up and find a mate. It wasn't like he wasn't looking—there just wasn't anyone he felt a spark with.

He wanted a woman he could form a connection with, someone who would be his equal in every way and he refused to settle. So he put up with the parade of potentials, smiled and subtly gritted his teeth.

An image flashed in his mind and it startled me.

Impossible.

A feeling of longing swept through him. This confused me because we had never met before and the image was from the dream I had the previous night. It appeared we'd shared the same dream.

Mason reached out his hand and pressed the doorbell again. He was intrigued by his dream, not knowing what it meant, and he couldn't get the picture of me out of his mind.

If only she was real, he mused.

The door swung open and I finally saw myself, the shock that registered on my face, but nothing—nothing compared to the overwhelming response that coursed through Mason. His entire body erupted into sensations, and his wolf clamored to be released.

Mine, it howled as it clawed to gain control. Mate.

My mind reeled as I sensed how stunned he was to find himself looking at his imagined dream girl and the rapid firing of his mind in trying to explain it. All the while, his wolf kept demanding for him to claim me.

He watched me stumble, concerned for my safety, and was again surprised at how natural it felt, his instinct to protect me. Already realizing the importance of the moment, he cringed as he heard himself speak.

Ugh. She must think I'm a moron. "Already

falling for me?" Jeez, could I be any cheesier?

Electricity pulsated over his skin as he grabbed hold of me and erotic images battered down on him hard. The two of us in a tight embrace, bed sheets twisted around our heated bodies as we touched and tasted each other. Him trapping me up against a wall, my legs wrapped around his waist as he took me over and over with fevered kisses as he all but consumed me. Scene after scene of all the things he was craving to do, and it caused my stomach to dip and body burn.

It wasn't just me who had felt that instant spark of desire, and I couldn't help chuckle over the war waging inside him as he fought to control himself.

I began to focus back on the present, pulling myself out of Mason's memory when I felt him tug me back in.

I'm not finished yet, Darcy. There's more.

A new scene opened up in my mind and I saw us sitting at dinner, Mason watching me as I chattered about a variety of random topics. I remembered how nervous I was, my hands flying everywhere as I spoke and wondering if he thought I was a complete idiot. Judging from the heat coursing through him, he not only thought I was the most adorable thing he had ever seen, but he was also desperately trying to control his need to wipe the table clean and have his way with me right there.

We always had that kind of intensity in our relationship, an overwhelming drive to take our fill of one another—which is one reason why we were always careful when we were together. One of the conditions in the mating ritual was the female should be pure for her mate. I always scoffed at the tradition because as werewolves we were driven by our basest desires, but my mother had drilled into me from birth the importance of me being a virgin. It hadn't really been an issue considering the losers I dated, but with Mason, we often walked a fine line. No sex for us, just incredibly hot make out sessions.

You were so beautiful. I couldn't keep my eyes off you. All I could think was, "She's all mine, how did I get so lucky?"

I was startled by his comment. I always believed I was the only one who thought that way. From the moment I'd seen him and as we got to know each other better, it was a reoccurring belief of mine as well. Sometimes I still pinched myself, just to make sure I wasn't dreaming and Mason was real.

It's funny how alike we think. I've thanked the Gods every day since for bringing you into my life. The sun rises and sets with you, Darcy. Always has and always will.

Back at the table, I watched as he gazed on me, every little detail catalogued for later reference. He took in the rich, thickness of my hair, the way it curled slightly, and how I tucked pieces of it behind my ears without thinking. He focused on my lips, the way they moved as I spoke. The shapes they made and the nervous way I licked them when I caught him staring.

Nothing was left unnoticed, every flaw I had was at his disposal.

No flaws Darcy. Just perfection, pure and simple.

He was captivated by me, enchanted by every nuance and the melodic sound of my voice. I felt him shake himself as if trying to ward off a spell. As the night continued, he fell harder and harder until he was completely consumed. There was no doubt about me being his mate and where I would fit into his life. He'd give everything up for me and would never let me go.

There has never been any question, even after everything that's happened. What do I need to do to convince you once and for all?

A shiver pulsated over my skin as his words echoed through my mind. The scene faded and I was brought back to the present. Our surroundings were surprisingly quiet and a peaceful feeling pervaded. The sun's heat tingled on my flesh and I felt Mason's embrace tighten slightly.

I closed my eyes and concentrated. I formed my answer in my mind, sending it to him along our pathway.

I believe you. Disappointment crashed over me as I realized my message hadn't gone through. There seemed to be an invisible wall that bounced my thoughts off and I was getting frustrated about how sporadic it worked.

Before Mason could say anything more, I turned around in his arms, feeling them slacken to accommodate my movements. I looked deep into his eyes and tried again.

I believe you. I pushed the thought from my mind to his and followed it with soft kiss to his lips. They were supple and tempting. I leaned back in for another, this time making it last longer.

There's something erotic about the stillness that comes to me when we share a kiss. Everything fades away until there's only me and him, hearts beating in anticipation. How his hot breath feels on my lips right before I quickly moisten them with my tongue. The flickering of his eyes as he breaks contact with mine so he can glance down at my mouth. I love the tingles that erupt over my skin, and how my stomach dips as if a million butterflies take flight. Everything inside screams for me to take what I want, to not draw it out, but seize the moment passionately. It doesn't matter how many times I kiss Mason, each time my reaction is the same. I'll never be able to get enough of the taste of him.

But my favorite moment is always the few seconds after I tenderly brush my lips against his, as I pull myself away with a slight smile.

What will he do? Will he take the bait?

Looking straight into his eyes, I prepared myself for it. The flash of hunger and desire that tells me he wants me just as bad, if not more. From the way his pupils dilate to the moment where I can almost see his wolf peering out through his eyes. One touch, that's all it ever takes.

Mason moved so fast if I'd blinked, I'd have missed it. His hand weaved its way through my hair, pulling my face back to his. The world stopped as he kissed me back. Forcefully. Masterfully. Perfectly.

I believe you, I repeated over and over as he dominated our kiss, his tongue stroking and moving against mine. I struggled not to drown in him as heat exploded in my body and I devoured everything he gave me. I poured all my love back into the moment, hoping I could somehow convey just how amazing I thought he was and how grateful I was for him. I couldn't tell him enough, show him enough, so I stopped trying and just reveled in the sensations I was experiencing. I was his and he was mine.

I couldn't help but quake as he brushed his fingers over my fevered skin, each touch wreaking havoc on my sensitive flesh, and I clung to him as our kiss deepened even more.

"You're killing me, Mason," I groaned helplessly into his mouth as I sunk into his embrace further. The man had turned me into a gooey mess.

His chuckle rumbled through his chest, vibrating against me, and he made to pull away. Whimpering, I moved to straddle him, taking control. Now he'd started, there was no way I was ready for it to be over.

Resting my hands on his shoulders, I dragged my nails down his skin, enjoying the way he convulsed under me. Just as he knew my weaknesses, I knew his and I planned on exploiting them thoroughly.

As he released a growl, I pulled back, bringing his bottom lip between my teeth and bit. Not hard enough to break skin, but enough to elicit another moan as his hands grabbed me by my hips, grinding me into his lap.

Like a red flag waving madly, the line we were forbidden to cross came painfully close and Mason seemed to sense it as well. Our bodies heaved in unison as I struggled to rein my passion in. I moved my hands lower to his chest, rubbing my fingertips in the fine layer of hair and daring myself to keep going south. His muscles rippled under my touch as I felt the firmness of his abdomen, the tension coiled just ready to snap.

I broke away, determined to taste what my fingers had found, leaving a trail as my tongue licked first his neck, then his shoulder.

Darcy. Stop. We can't .... His thought cut off as my mouth found his chest. I moved backward so I could have better access and found myself suddenly pinned to the ground. My hands were firmly held by the side of my head with Mason lying squarely on top of me. I snapped my teeth at him, tempting him to play more.

He lowered his head down and rested it against mine. The fever so quickly roused had left us breathless, and we took a few moments to cool off. I wiggled slightly under him, the friction igniting the fire all over again and the next thing I knew, he threw me over his shoulder, and headed for the water.

"Hey, put me down," I shouted, beating against his

back when he ignored me.

A firm hand landed on my behind, swatting me as Mason finally reached the pool's edge.

"You need to cool off, my little vixen." He laughed before unceremoniously dumping me in the water. I spluttered to the surface, my hair a wet, tangled mess. Even through the strands, I could see the smirk on his face.

I submerged myself back under, moving towards the edge where he stood. I shot out into the air, droplets spraying everywhere and latched onto his arm. With a grin of my own, I yanked on his wrist and watched him soar over my head and land behind me. The splash it created left me spitting out water.

I turned around to confront him, but he was nowhere to be seen. I stared at the ripples covering the surface and realized the sneak was trying to surprise me. With a grin, I readied my stance.

A few moments past and there was still nothing. No break whatsoever. No goofy Mason. I began turning and turning, trying to see where he was. Just as I thought my heart was about to burst from my chest, I heard the whisper.

"BOO." This mammoth form rose from the depths and crushed me to it, face first.

"Ugh, you scared me!" I screamed, hitting his chest. A fleeting shot of pain pulsed through my palm. Damn, it was like hitting a brick wall.

"You cooled off yet, baby?" he said with a grin, using his hand to wipe away the excess droplets. He looked like a god, standing there dripping wet, muscles flexing as he moved his hair out from his eyes. He must've seen my intent because he suddenly pushed me away, his arm held out to stop me as I moved toward him. I sent the theme song to

Jaws through our pathway as I stalked him in the water. He must have received it because he started laughing.

"Enough of that now, Darcy. You still have questions, remember? Focus a little and maybe I'll play with you later." He winked at me before sending a small wave at me. I raised myself up, avoiding the splash to my face. I sent one back in return and he dipped himself under the pool's surface.

Not to be caught a second time, I pushed off the bottom with my feet and swam into the center. It was deep, but not enough to cause me to panic.

It was a myth werewolves abhorred all forms of water. Like anybody else, there were definitely some of us who had a fear of drowning, but for the most part, we enjoyed a good swim. Right now, it felt cool against my heated skin.

Not paying any attention to Mason, I leaned back and began to float, allowing my arms to gently caress through the crystal liquid, enjoying the feeling of weightlessness. There was something calming about being suspended and I closed my eyes, tuning everything else out.

Chapter Eight

He must have realized I needed this moment because he didn't come after me, leaving me to my thoughts.

My feelings were definitely different from this morning. Gone was the need to run and hide from him. While the grief for Jasmine was still there, a constant weight around my heart, he had convinced me we would be okay, and nothing had changed between us. I took great comfort in that and wrapped it around me like a warm, fluffy blanket, fresh out of the dryer. I took strength from knowing I wasn't alone, and I would always have my strong wolf mate beside me. A contented sigh escaped my lips. The pain I was feeling would lessen over time. There were still matters to take care of and within the month—finally, our mating ritual.

In the few short hours since I'd been awake, I felt lighter and I knew I owed it all to Mason. When the man set out to prove a point, he never held back, and I was grateful once again for his devotion. He could've easily used his Alpha powers to command me to see sense. Maybe a lesser person would've, but not him. He always lead with his heart when it came to me, never afraid to show just how deeply he felt. It was one of the many things I loved about him.

A cold breeze wafted over my skin, and I

realized I couldn't feel the sun anymore. I opened my eyes slowly, seeing it crest through the trees and I recognized time had passed. We'd pushed the limits of Devlin's patience long enough, and standing up, I looked around for Mason.

He was reclining against a crop of rocks, catching the last of the sun's rays before it dipped fully behind the tree line. He stole my breath with his masculine beauty, the way the light played off the golden tint of his skin. Moisture collected in my mouth as I waded my way over to him, careful not to disturb him. There weren't many moments where he was able to just relax and I loved seeing the boyish look of peace covering his face.

Reaching up, I went to trail my fingers over his abdomen, wanting to see them tense when his hand whipped out and grabbed hold of my wrist.

"No you don't, Darcy. No touching. We need to head back. I can feel everyone going crazy back at the house."

For someone who should be moving, Mason lay still, his eyes closed. He could've been asleep if it wasn't for the wide grin he was wearing. He lifted my hand to his mouth, gently kissing the back of it and slowly pulled himself into a sitting position.

My hungry eyes took in every move, and I was pretty sure I sighed.

"I love the way you move. Are you sure we have to go back straight away?" I tried to put a smolder in the look I gave him, but Mason was busy stretching out his muscles, looking around.

"I'm glad I brought you here. I like the idea that this is something special—just for us. I have lots of plans involving this place." He smiled, wiggling his eyebrows at me.

He moved slowly, leisurely over to a pair of trees,

looking behind it for something.

What are you looking for? I whispered mentally to him. Nothing. Not even an indication he'd heard me. Mason? I tried harder. It was like talking to myself.

Hey Mason, I think we should run away and raise cows and bunnies and all things rainbow and sunshine. I shouted mentally, focusing as hard as I could while sending images.

That made him pause. He slowly stopped, a look of curiosity on his face. "Rainbow cows dancing with bunnies in the sun? Something you want to share?"

I rolled my eyes at him. Obviously, whatever was happening with the mental connection between us, it was distorting things. I watched him look one more time around the trees before giving up and walking back over to me.

"I was trying to ask you what you were looking for, but I don't think you were hearing me." I laughed, folding my arms across my chest. This really was starting to irritate me because it shouldn't be so difficult. Heck, a child could learn something this fundamentally simple, but I was struggling. It didn't make sense. Mason's thoughts came through loud and clear every time, just not mine.

He looked a little distracted. "I was trying to remember where I put some of my clothes I like to stash in cases of emergencies. As much as I love looking at you naked, I'm not too keen about flaunting your curves to everyone."

"Especially Devlin, huh?" I interrupted with a wink.

Mason grumbled at my response. "Especially the vampire." He slapped my butt as he passed me by, heading in the direction of the house. I stood there, still as a statue as the flaming heat in my bottom tingled. Dang that man, he knew what that did to me.

He paused and turned around, lifting his arm out to me. "Come on—back to reality."

I reached out, taking his hand in mine and squeezed. He was already starting to resume the look of an Alpha.

People laughed at me whenever I said Mason had different looks. To them, he always appeared the same, but to me he had a softer, more playful side that he showed to very few. Then there was what I liked to call the don't-mess-with-me look, where you could feel the leadership mantle he carried crackling in the air like magic. Both were sexy as hell, but when he added the mischievous smirk and wicked glint in his eyes, I was a goner.

We started walking, side by side in comfortable silence. It didn't last for long, however, as he let out a full chuckle. I couldn't help look and feel a warm tingly feeling in the bottom of my stomach. I loved watching him laugh.

"So you ever going to explain those images you sent me, or do I not want to know?"

I wouldn't be surprised if he already knew what was going on—the man had a sixth sense when it came to me. I can't count how many arguments I've tried to have with him where I said, "Why do I even bother telling you anything. You can just read my mind and find out!" Depending on what happened, I'd add a healthy foot stomp to my anger.

He was always gentle in his reply, calmly reminding me he would never purposely invade my privacy like that.

"It gets a little scary how quiet you are at times. But there are moments when you think so dang loud, you're shouting," he added with a grin.

Seemed the key to my connection was doing it without forcing it, because whenever I tried to purposely send something, it got lost or mixed up.

I sighed heavily, hoping I'd be able to figure it out. Something told me things were about to get even more crazy, and I needed to know I could rely on it.

"Mason, why doesn't our connection always work?" I blurted out as we continued walking. "Sometimes it's crystal clear, I hear you and you hear me, but there other times when it's like talking to a brick wall. It scares me that if I ever need you like last night, it will fail again."

He seemed to take his time responding as he searched for an answer to ease my anxiety. "I'm not sure what's happening, but I agree we need to figure out why so we can fix it. It might be related to our mating ritual being incomplete, but my gut tells me it's something else."

"My gut tells me something is wrong with me. I'm broken and it worries me because it makes me feel like I'm less of a wolf. I grew up hearing about how wonderful the link between mates is and watching others enjoy their silent conversations. What if we never have that?"

"You're not broken, Darcy. But if it helps, when this business with Devlin and the vampire blood is resolved, I'll send for Vivien and see if she knows anything. You can't be the only wolf this has happened to. We'll get to the bottom of it, babe."

I loved Vivien. She was the leader of the local witch coven everyone went to when they had questions—her magic undeniably powerful. She was an incredible wealth of knowledge on all things supernatural, fully versed in all kinds of myths and legends. If there was anyone who could solve this, it was her.

"I hope so because it was terrifying last night when I tried talking and I didn't know if you were going to come. I felt so alone and helpless. I don't know what I would've done if you hadn't arrived when you did." I stopped dead in my tracks, a hint of curiosity in my voice. "Actually, how did you know we needed you? One minute I couldn't sense you and then there you were."

Mason stroked his hand through his hair, causing it to spike a little and make it look messy. A look of anger flashed in his eyes and it was now his turn to pace.

"I can't begin to describe how frustrating it was. One moment I was in the kitchen cooking you a surprise dinner, and next this overwhelming sense of urgency and fear coursed through me. It was like nothing I'd ever experienced, and frankly, I never want to again. I could feel my wolf banging against my skin like a fierce warrior ready to fight, his howl like a battle cry in my ears. I had no way of knowing what it meant, just that it was from you and you were terrified. I almost ripped Daniel to shreds when he walked into the room, I was that feral. I wasn't getting any words or clear sentences—just a lot of emotions. It wasn't until I stopped and focused that I started getting images. That's when all hell broke loose."

I rubbed the side of my arms, as if warding off the cold, and walked into Mason's embrace. "I'm sorry," I whispered.

I knew he hated feeling helpless and this must've been extremely painful. It would've gone against every instinct he had—wanting to rush out and protect me, but not having any directions.

"It took Daniel a few minutes and a level head to help me see reason again. Darcy, I've always been able to keep calm in a crisis. It's what makes me a formidable opponent and great Alpha. But seeing images of a gun and feeling your fear, it almost drove me insane."

"All the more reason for us to figure out what's happening with the connection, right?" I felt him nod against the top of my head.

"We finally decided to jump in the car and patrol the streets between here and the store, trusting you'd keep to your usual route. I had Daniel and the boys come with me and sent the others to circle around in case we missed you. I could feel the change in emotions when you shifted and your wolf took over. She's amazing, Darcy, truly. I've never felt such sheer determination and courage. It was only then I was able to relax and think clearly."

"I don't know what I would've done without her, Mason. I can't help wondering if I had let her out sooner, would everything have turned out differently. Jasmine would be here and ...."

He lifted my chin and tilted my head back. "Shhh. We're not going through that again, remember? What happened, happened and all the "what if's" in the world won't change it. Focus on the fact you survived and were able to bring Gary to justice for Jasmine. She can rest easy now."

"How can you do that?" I asked skeptically.

"Do what?" Mason replied as his brows furrowed.

"Talk about Jasmine's death as if it doesn't hurt."

Suddenly his hand flashed, becoming wolf-like before quickly changing back to human. I looked at it stunned because although I knew he had the power to partially change, I'd never seen him lose control like that. Staring up into his face, it still held a wolfish quality with his mouth turned into a snarl, revealing razor sharp fangs. His eyes blazed with a fury that made me stagger back slightly from their intensity.

The air sizzled with electricity and magic. Our surroundings suddenly became frightfully quiet as if all the animals and birds sensed the immediate danger.

The strain on his face was painfully visible as I watched him struggle to control his change. It caused my own wolf to howl and chomp as she pushed to join her mate. I'd never felt anything so severe and concentrated from him before and it broke my heart.

All this time, he'd focused on me, making sure I was okay with what happened and all the while he was dying inside. I pushed out my senses and almost crumpled under the bombardment of excruciating pain and grief. Tears began to streak down my cheek again as I watched my beloved Mason battle for his sanity.

Chapter Nine

I stretched out to touch him, my fingers tingling from the energy pulsating off his skin. I caressed him and cooed softly, trying to help him find his balance.

He fought a little against my attempts, but gradually, we were able to calm the savageness of his beast to the point where he was completely human. He stood there, angry and defeated, his head hung low with his fists clenching slightly. He was still on edge, but nowhere near as volatile. Had he decided to leave earlier, I shuddered to think the damage he would've done to anyone foolish enough to get in his way.

I stooped a little to catch his gaze, sweeping the strands of his hair away from his eyes. This man was just so magnificent, and I wanted nothing more than to take this from him. It was only now, as we stood in silence, I realized the full weight of his responsibilities as Alpha, and what astonishing strength it took him to maintain his calm façade. It also made me wonder just how much he hid from the world—or even me.

"Talk to me, Mason. Please." I took him by the hand and lifted it to my heart. "Let me in." I stared in amazement as a solitary tear streaked down his cheek. His eyes were rapidly filling, and I watched as he fought to clamp down hard on his emotions and push out a stoic expression.

"Don't you dare try to hide yourself from me. Talk to me. Yell, rage and cry. Anything but shut me out!" I released his hand and placed my own on his chest. I could feel the violent pounding of his heart and the deep sobs that were churning inside. He was ready to explode and with what we were about to face, I knew he couldn't afford to lose this battle.

Had I not been standing so close, I would've missed his whispered reply. "I'm a failure."

The sound of despair and anguish was soul crushing and sent my mind reeling.

"What ...?" I couldn't even finish the sentence, the idea was so beyond my understanding. Here stood the most courageous man I'd ever been blessed to know. He was so selfless, putting everyone's needs before his own, making himself available to help anyone who needed him. I'd seen a few Alphas up close during my life and none of them came close to the kind of integrity and honor Mason showed. He went far beyond, seeing his role as more than just a job, but a calling. He was fair, honest, and loyal to a fault. You couldn't look at him and doubt he gave everything. How he thought he was a failure stumped me.

"I thought you accepted there was nothing more you could've done, that the true villain was Gary. Or was it just a line to calm me?" I asked, not caring I was throwing his words back at him.

Mason drew in a deep breath, as if trying to pull his thoughts from the air. "I'm just waiting for my heart to catch up, Darcy. That's all."

"Then we'll talk about it. Tell me what's happening here." I gently tapped his chest again. "And don't say "nothing" because this doesn't feel like everything is fine."

More tears began to stream down his cheeks, and

he raised his fist to rub them away. "No, we need to get back and take care of business." He put steel into his voice and went to move me, but I refused to budge.

"Oh no, you don't. You wanted to talk so we're not going anywhere until I know you're okay." I added a stern edge to my voice. "Don't make me order you."

He snorted loudly at that. "With what authority, Darcy? Last time I checked, I was the Alpha here."

"The if-you-don't-talk-you'll-spend-an-eternity-sleeping-on-the-couch kind of authority, Your Royal Grouchy Pants." I slapped his bare chest for emphasis. "Don't be a jerk, you know what I mean."

That earned me a small soft smile and it warmed me. "I can't afford to go into this right now. We'll deal with it later." He moved again to pull me toward the house.

"No, we'll deal now." I dug my heels into the ground.

"Why are you being so stubborn about this, Darcy?" He demanded hotly, fire lighting in his eyes.

"Stubborn? Isn't that like the pot calling the kettle black?" I retorted, my hands resting on my hips to match my attitude. "You, Mister I-won't-talk-about-it, are the epitome of stubbornness. Now spill."

"No."

"You did not just deny me." My own temper began to rise.

"Please, Darcy, I know what you're trying to do, but just let it be. I can't." The pleading in his voice pierced me and I avoided looking into his eyes.

"You can't what? Confide in your mate? Explain

why you think this is your fault? Share how you feel?" I threw my questions rapidly at him. "You asked me to trust you knew what we needed, and I did. You were right, so I'm asking the same. You need this now. Until you share the burden you're holding onto, you're going to be off balanced. Let me help you carry it. Trust me."

"I can't be weak!" he shouted and it sent a flurry of birds flying into the air as the words exploded from his mouth. "Damn it, Darcy. I have to go into that meeting soon and make decisions which heavily affect not just us, but the entire Pack, and you want me talking about my feelings?"

"How does that make you weak? Do you think people are going to think less of you because you grieve? You lost your sister, Mason. You almost lost me. If that's not grounds to show a little vulnerability, I don't know what else is. No one expects you to be perfect either."

"They don't?" he scoffed. "I have the constant attention of the power hungry, who look for the slightest chink in my armor so they can exploit it. I may rule this Pack, but there are always people willing to claw their way to the top. How am I supposed to keep you safe if I have to ward off challenges?"

"Now you're starting to sound like me, and if I remember right, you told me all you ever expected was for me to be myself. I say take your own advice. Allow yourself at least a few moments to feel before you shut it all off. It's not healthy. And answer me honestly, are you going to be able to keep focused when inside you're divided? That hurt and pain you're burying requires energy to stay that way. Wouldn't it be better to release some of the pressure so you don't feel so tightly wound."   I rested my ear to his chest, stroking him with my fingers. "It sounds intense in there, Mason—chaotic, and I need you to trust me now. Let some of it go if you can't free all of it. Just do something because it's killing me to see you like this."

He thrummed under my touch, and I felt the subtle change in his body. He relaxed ever so slightly and then it seemed like he shattered. Choking sobs blasted out of him, and he dropped to the floor, holding his head in his hands as he wept.

I said nothing as I joined him, gathering him into my arms so I could shelter him. To be so strong for so long was a burden and I was honored at the trust he showed by revealing how devastated he was. I know I'd told him it was okay to be vulnerable, but I understood just how against the grain it was for him to be in this state. I feathered little kisses over the top of his head and held on tight.

The depths of his emotions were profound and seemed to go on without end. I murmured over and over it was okay and he must have found it amusing because he offered a rather cynical chuckle.

Pulling himself back up, he lifted his head to look at me. "How is this okay? What kind of leader and mate will I be if I can't even protect my sister? Yes, I know rationally it's not my fault," he said, cutting me off before I could interrupt him. "It just kills me I wasn't there. I watched my father be this controlling, dominating force in our family growing up. He ruled with an iron fist and too bad if you didn't like it. It didn't matter who it was, if you questioned him, he'd beat you back into submission. My mother had absolutely no freedom and it pained me to see her put up with his abusiveness because she was afraid for her children. My father was a monster in every sense of the word and I vowed ... vowed, Darcy, I would never become like him."

"But you're not. You are far from that," I gently added.

"I'm not?" He choked, sarcasm heavy in his voice. "You have no idea how hard it is sometimes not to lock you in your room and never let you out—to watch your independence and not move to stifle it. It makes me crazy with worry I'll lose you because I don't trust myself if I did. It would infuriate Jasmine whenever we argued because our ideas on protecting were so different. Even now, part of me is raging over my foolishness. If I'd stopped fighting my nature, Jasmine would still be here. So you see? This is my fault—my weakness and my cross to bear."

"It's not your fault and we'll bear this together," I answered, pulling him back into my embrace. My fingers found his hair and I began to tenderly stroke his head.

"I let her down." He sobbed again, his body convulsing. Anguish poured off him and I quietly let him vent.

"I miss her so much. Her smile, the way she used to say my name when I teased her. You never realize just how much someone means to you until they're gone. What devastates me is I never got to say goodbye. I don't even think I told her I loved her when you both left. I thought there was plenty of time and now I feel cheated and angry. Gary stole from me … from us. There are so many things I'll never be able to do with my baby sister because of a man's obsession with something he couldn't have." He took a deep breath in between his outbursts before continuing. "She told me about the dreams she'd been having of a man she didn't recognize. Dreams where he told her he was her mate and he was coming for her. She didn't know what the meant, and needed to know what her big brother thought about it."

I'd forgotten about her dream. Mason and I had always thought she'd mate with Daniel, the childhood crush she'd carried for him still strong even through the years. Jasmine had been so excited to share the next morning, and we'd spent time day dreaming over the possibilities, imagining what the mystery wolf would be life.

His eyes widen as he remembered. "You should've seen the way her eyes sparkled, Darcy. She could barely contain her excitement, bouncing around in her seat like she was about to explode. We must have talked for an hour as she asked me question after question. Who did I think he was? Where was he? Could she trust the dream? I couldn't help laughing, her enthusiasm was so addicting. I teased her about Daniel, telling her how this would crush him, but you could tell the idea of her settling down intrigued her. I don't know if it will ever come to past, but what if it was true? Am I supposed to wait for that future knock on the door and have to share with a stranger the woman he was expecting is gone?" His voice broke. "No happily ever after for her. No babies ... no future. All gone in the blink of an eye."

I tried to speak, but couldn't. My own tears coursed down my face as I listened to him bare his soul.

"I don't ever want to fail like that again. I need to be strong so I should forewarn you, don't kill me if I start to get a little possessive and over protective. I don't mean to, but I'm fighting instincts here. Be patient."

"Whatever you need, I love you. And Jasmine ... she was so proud of you," I whispered when I finally found my voice. "You're a good man. Don't ever doubt it."

We huddled together in silence, caught up in the truthfulness of the moment. Gone was the thrumming and buildup of magic. The aggression and anger from before had also abated and I could sense his fatigue. I don't think he realized just how much he had bottled until he pulled the cork and let it out.

"Was that good enough?" he chuckled, his body putty under my hands. "I didn't scare you away with my sappiness?" I could sense the mood changing as he began to bring himself back together.

"Never. You're stuck with me forever." I leaned forward and kissed him lightly.

"Good, because I'd accept nothing less. I love you, Darcy." He smiled and this time it reached his eyes. "And thank you. I'll admit, I do feel better and not so heavy inside."

"Then that's all that matters. You're not alone anymore. You have me and I will always be here to listen. We strengthen each other and there's nothing to be ashamed of in needing a little help. There's no weakness in it." I made sure to put emphasis on the last part. I didn't want him walking away thinking I felt he was less of a man because he'd shown his emotions.

"I hear you." He slowly pulled himself up and reached down to lift me. "Ugh."

I looked at him. "I hope that ugh wasn't referring to the fact you think I'm heavy." I raised my eyebrow at him, waiting.

"No, even I'm not that stupid." He laughed as he dodged the swing of my arm. "It's Daniel. He's almost frantic wondering where we are."

We helped dust each other off, brushing away pieces of leaves and dirt. I heard the movement of a rabbit, hopping through the foliage and noted the sounds of the woods had returned. The crisis had been averted.

Walking back in the direction of the house, we swung our arms between us as we held hands. I looked down at our fingers entwined together, and couldn't help but smile. Yep, we were okay.

I flashed him some images of what else I wanted to see entwined, expecting to get a response, but Mason looked like he was enjoying his surroundings. I added a little heat to my thoughts, sending them back along the pathway and was rewarded with that sexy smile I loved so much.

"Really? You promise?" he questioned, his temperature spiking with arousal.

"And then some." I sent him a new image that caused even me to blush.

When I got no reaction, I sighed heavily. I was getting tired of how sporadic my connection with him was acting. One thing I noticed was it was practically flawless when I was in close proximity to him while in wolf form. It kind of made sense, but it wasn't good enough. Seeing we spent most of our day and night as humans, I really needed it to work perfectly each and every time.

I gasped as an idea flashed through my mind and fear rushed through me. Please, please don't make that be why.

"What if my connection problem is because we're mismatched?" I blurted out.

"Mismatched?" he asked, a confused look on his face.

"Yeah, what happens if I got the wrong wolf? What if she was supposed to go to someone else and there was some big cosmic mix up?" I knew I sounded delusional, but at this point I was clutching at straws.

Mason ran his fingers through my hair,

separating some of the strands now they were drying. "Baby, it doesn't work like that, remember? Each of us are born with a wolf that is unique to us, one who brings us balance and helps us be complete. There is no such thing as mix ups, wrong deliveries, or whatever. You and your wolf were destined to be together. You strengthen and help one another when the other is weak. I'm sure if you asked her, she'd tell you the same thing. It's a soul connection that can't be denied or replicated. There's something else at work here."

"Okay." I couldn't help the way my voice wavered with uncertainty.

He brought my gaze back to his and kissed me softly. "Trust me."

"Okay. I love you."

"I love you too," he replied before deepening the kiss.

I sank into Mason, reveling in how amazing his lips felt against mine. I don't know how long we stood there, caught up in the moment, but when he finally broke away, I was a little lightheaded. I grinned at the idea I was becoming a swooning werewolf.

"You ready to face the music? Daniel says Devlin is there and he's getting more and more impatient. For someone who's immortal and has all eternity before him, he doesn't care for being made to wait. Apparently some of the younger cubs have locked themselves in their rooms because they said he was staring at their necks."

I laughed at the image in my mind, of the devilishly handsome vampire licking his fangs at them. It was exactly something the teasing Enforcer would do.

"Poor things. Hasn't anyone told them he's just a big softy?"

"Only around you, Darcy. From the images Daniel showed me, it was too funny so everyone there just let them go. He's gathered the others so we can start the meeting." He chuckled. "We good?" He peered down into my eyes.

"We're more than good. Race you back to the house." And I took off running.

Chapter Ten

I couldn't stop smiling at the sense of freedom I felt, even though I knew what lay ahead of me. This time with Mason had truly been an elixir to my soul and helped restore a lot of the confidence I'd lost. My feet flew across the ground as I tried to watch for holes and fallen logs. The last thing I needed was to stumble and injure something.

I expected him to pass me because he was definitely the faster of us both, and when I didn't hear him coming, I figured he liked the "view" better from where he was. I tried to put a little wiggle as I moved, but when I almost fell, I gave up sexy for speed. Problem was I still wasn't hearing him behind me. He was stealthy, but not so good he could move without making a sound.

I came to a complete stop and whipped around, my hair flying everywhere and I had to take a moment to pull it away from my face. All I could see was forest. No Mason.

A black wolf flew through a batch of low hanging leaves and I realized that the rotten punk was cheating. It reminded me when challenging a werewolf; make sure I was specific because they'll look for any loophole to win. I hadn't said how we'd race home so he changed into his wolf form, having the ultimate advantage. There was no way in heck

I'd beat him unless I quickly shifted myself.

I worried it would take longer to change this time. All the shifting of muscle and bone takes a toll on the body and where magic alleviates most of the strain, there was a limit to just how much it could do.

I reached out to my wolf, getting a sense of how she was feeling. I expected some sort of lethargic energy, but she was rearing to go. I puzzled over it, and discerned a power I knew instantly as Mason's. He was channeling some of his own Alpha power to me, lending me the strength so I could catch up. I didn't quite understand the gist of it all, but being Alpha came with some pretty amazing abilities and I couldn't wait to learn more about them.

I signaled quietly to my wolf that we could change and felt the process begin. It happened rapidly this time and before I knew it, I was barreling as fast as I could after Mason, quickly gaining on him. It didn't take a rocket scientist to know he was pacing himself, not really exerting much of an effort.

With a howl of exuberance, I breezed past him, my tongue lolling out the side of my mouth as if to mock him and I kicked up dirt in my eagerness to beat him home. I could hear him pick up speed when he realized I stood a real chance and knowing he'd never live it down, he almost caught up.

You're a cheater Mason O'Connor. I laughed as I sent a scandalous image to him with my mind. There was a loud bang behind me and a quick glance told me my trick had worked. Mason was a tangled ball of paws and fur, having ran into the gate that secured the property. That'd teach him to mess with me.

That was a dirty trick, Darcy.

Well, I've learned from the best. First one home gets all the hot water.

I broke into the yard and entered the house to the

squealing of everyone I passed. It wasn't unusual to see the young cubs in wolf form, playing around, but not so much the older wolves.

"No running in the house, you two," Daniel bellowed as I barged past him, almost pushing him back over the chair. "Oh I'm sorry, Your Most Impressive Duke of All Things Furry. Proceed as you will," he directed at the wolf directly behind me. His comment almost undid me as I imagined the face Mason would've pulled had he been human.

A yelp of pain and a rapid burst of cussing told me he'd taught the irreverent jokester a lesson in manners, and I was able to make it into my room with moments to spare. The shift back took seconds.

A snout became visible around the door way, and I rushed forward with the intention of slamming the door and locking it before Mason could enter. Somehow I managed and I leaned back against the hard surface, gasping for breath.

The door handle rattled as I felt someone pounding against the door. "Let me in, Darcy. That wasn't a fair race so I deserve to have the shower first." He beat on the entry again for extra emphasis.

"Fine then, go to one of the other four bathrooms. Heaven knows, we don't have to share." The idea of bathing with Mason after the passion stirred earlier started a slow burn in my body. I shook my head as I moved away toward the bathroom entrance. I had no idea how we would last until the mating ritual.

"Now go be a good wolf and get changed so we can take care of business. Leave me in peace and I'll meet you outside in ten minutes." Judging from the silence on the other side of the wall, Mason had already moved on, seeking his own shower.

Nerves began to twist in my stomach as I closed over the curtain and turned the faucets on, testing the temperature with my right hand. The water was hot and the room quickly filled with steam. I let out a loud groan as the beating of the heated spray started to melt away the tension.

I began to scrub my hair, lathering it up with my favorite scented shampoo, and with my eyes closed, I reached for the loofah. Not finding it hanging where I usually placed it, I began feeling around and gasped when I found something unexpected.

"All the other bathrooms were taken," Mason's voice was low and rumbly. I felt him move slightly then begin to scrub my back. He applied just the right amount of pressure and I let out another groan of appreciation. He moved down to the base of my back before crouching down to wash my legs.

"We don't have time for this. Any longer, they'll send out a search party, Devlin in the lead."

"No need to panic." He laughed, taking the time to apply more of my favorite body wash and creating suds. "Just let me wash you up. It's about me taking care of you and one last chance to pamper my beautiful mate. I want no doubt in that mind of yours how much you're loved."

I grinned at him, careful not to get soap in my eyes and relaxed into him, enjoying the feel of his strong hands moving me about as he tended to me.

"Repeat after me. I am loved and I am cherished."

I opened my eyes to peer at him and I met with a serious expression.

"Come on, say it."

I took a deep breath and sighed. "I am loved, and I am cherished."

"Good. Now turn around and let me get your front."

It didn't take too long after that before he had me wrapped in a large towel as he rubbed me dry before pushing me back into the bedroom. I quickly grabbed a pair of faded jeans and t-shirt, a comfortable silence between us. After running a brush through my hair, I turned around to find him ready with his game face on.

Silently, we exited and headed toward his office, hand in hand. With each step we took, I could feel a different kind of change come over us. I mentally prepared myself for the questions that would be asked and for the memories that would resurface as I retold the story. I prayed I would remember it all and not leave out any important detail. I was scared about what it all meant, but as I looked at the fierce Alpha beside me, I knew I'd be okay.

Mason's expression lost all playfulness as a seriousness settled over him. Decisions would have to be made and I knew he worried about the safety of the Pack. It was up to him to make sure everything was okay, and that any threat to him and his own be quickly exterminated. He didn't like violence, but accepted it as a natural part of his life.

We reached the door, but as I went to move forward, Mason stopped me.

"Remember. It's you and me—there's nothing we can't get through together. Take your time and don't let anybody bully you. Do the best you can and know I'm proud of you." He quickly kissed me before pushing open the door. The noise of the room hushed and I heard everyone rise to their feet in respect for their Alpha.

Taking a deep breath, I centered myself. I am

loved and I am cherished. I could do this.

Empowered, I walked through the doorway and smiled. I was ready. Bring it on.

Chapter Eleven

The power in the room had me thrumming the very second I entered, sliding over my skin and a shiver coursed through me. It was the same reaction I had each time I was surrounded by some of the most dominant males in the pack. Separately, each of them was a pussy cat. Together, they were lethal.

I looked around and my chest tightened— Daniel, Eric, Jonas, and Wade. I loved each of my brothers and the look of concern covering their faces shared just how much the events of last night had shaken them. It was one thing to go up against a pack male, another completely when threatening one of the females.

I walked past each one of them, letting my hand touch them briefly, giving them a chance to see I was in fact safe and in one piece. I couldn't give them Jasmine, and it hurt, but now wasn't the time for that.

As I took my seat next to Mason, who was all Alpha authority now, I looked around and took note of the other faces in the meeting. Devlin was sitting a few seats down, and I was pretty confident he hadn't taken his gaze off me the entire time I'd been in the room. His stare was intense, as though he was trying to penetrate the wall of protection I'd erected and see into the heart of the matter.

For a vampire enforcer, someone who lived a life of justice and violence, I had a special kind of relationship with him. I smiled as my eyes met his. He nodded in return and I knew I hadn't fooled him. It always impressed me how much he could communicate without ever saying a word. Sometime in the next few days Devlin would want to talk with me, and I bowed my head in return, letting him know to come find me.

There was someone new sitting by him, and judging by the way he drummed his fingers against the table, he wasn't used to being in a room with this many werewolves. I leaned forward, trying to discern what kind of supernatural being he was because surely a vampire wouldn't give away such an obvious tell of nervousness. Smelling the air, I reclined back shocked.

Vampire. Taking in his appearance and the way he held himself, I would say newly turned because there was no way an older one would throw off such a strong scent of uncertainty. I caught Devlin's eye, gesturing towards his companion, and I was rewarded with a slight fanged grin. He rolled his eyes and shook his head.

Reaching out, he placed his hand over the nervous vampire's and brought the agitation to a standstill. I'm not sure what was whispered between the two, but the look on the young man's face was priceless as he blanched and visibly straightened in his chair. I tried not to giggle when Devlin turned to me and winked. There was a story there, one I couldn't wait to uncover.

"Is everyone here?"

All eyes focused on Mason as he stood by his chair, waiting to bring the meeting to a start. If I thought the intensity of power in the room was overwhelming before, now it was stifling. Yes, these were men, but I was also surrounded by predators—hunters desperate for retribution and answers.

The air crackled and each body instantly tensed. Placing my hand gently on Mason's leg, he looked down at me and smiled.

"By now, you would've all heard about the attack last night," he paused, his voice cracking slightly. "Jasmine was taken from us, but thankfully, Darcy was able to take care of the situation and return to us safely."

All heads turned my way and I struggled not to flinch or sink deep into my chair. Stiffening my spine, I met everyone's gaze before returning to Mason.

"Not all of us are familiar with the events." The voice belonged to the vampire newbie, and he wasn't able to hide his cringe when the full focus swung to him. I think he even squeaked the next part of his sentence before remembering where, and what, he was. "I'd appreciate hearing the account from Darcy herself."

"Who the hell are you to ask anything?" The question came from Wade, one of the younger pack members, and a gentle hand on the shoulder from Eric reminded him that outbursts wouldn't go down well.

"I'm Vlad, and I come on behalf of my king to see how we may assist." There was a hint of indignation in his voice as he sat up taller, seemingly developing his courage. "I accompany Devlin today to determine whether last night was an isolated event or something more." Having finished his speech he leaned back, looking proud he'd been able to spit out the mouthful.

There was a brief second of confusion as each pack member glanced up toward Mason for direction, but before he could respond Wade burst into laughter, his throaty chuckle mocking.

"Vlad? Are you kidding me? Who the hell names you damn vampires? Don't tell me, your last name is "the Impaler?" He shook his head, and seemed confused when Eric's hand returned to his shoulder, this time with a more visible squeeze. The message was clear—shut up or he would do it for him.

"What? Seriously, you don't think this is even remotely funny? We're here to discuss what happened, and Mr. Dracula wannabe over there is speaking like he has a say in anything that goes on here. It's a joke." Wade slammed his body back against his chair, blowing out a breath of disgust. "Why are they even here?" He glared hard towards Devlin and Vlad.

"Wade, you'll learn to curb your tongue, or find your ass tossed out of this meeting. I saw potential in you, an opportunity to bring you into pack business, but if you can't control yourself, there's the door." Even I was surprised by the edge in Mason's voice. He didn't show his temper, but everyone knew he wouldn't be pushed.

"Sorry." The apology came out as a quiet murmur. Slouching down in his seat, Wade looked embarrassed to be called out in front of everyone. After a few moments, attention shifted from the chastised wolf back to the Alpha.

The room was silent, waiting to see what happened next, and a quick cough interrupted the pause.

"Maybe I should step in now?" Devlin said, and you never would've thought anything was wrong judging from the relaxed way he held himself. We could've been discussing the weather for all he revealed. Only those who knew him, who knew what to look for, could sense any kind of agitation from him. He was the master of concealment.

I watched him stand, pushing back the chair, and give a slight bow to those around the table. Always one to offer small tokens of respect, Devlin showed his age as he placed his hand over his heart and extended his condolences.

"First, may I speak on behalf of Zane, my King and share how deeply disturbed we were to hear about last night and the profound affected it's had on your pack. It pained him to learn vampire blood was involved and he has sent me to provide whatever assistance you may need to uncover the truth. I'm therefore at your disposal and carry the authority of my liege."

Devlin turned his focus to me and I couldn't help but flush at what I found in his eyes. To everyone else, they were bottomless pools of black, but I saw fury, compassion and concern.

"Darcy, please accept the relief felt by our people to know you are safe and unharmed. We too hold our females in high esteem, and the way you dealt with the threat shows the incredible woman you are. You bring great honor to your pack as a warrior of worth."

I was stunned by his declaration and almost missed the slight wink he offered.

Lastly, facing Mason, Devlin bowed again, and his voice took on a hint of sorrow. "Mason, Alpha of the Mystic Wolves, please accept the deepest of regrets for the loss of your sister, Jasmine. She truly was a beautiful creature, and the world is a darker place for having lost her. My liege understands there's nothing that can replace her, but asks for you to notify him should he be able to help in any way. He has two beloved sisters himself, and the news has stirred him greatly."

Mason's hand squeezed mine as we listened to the Enforcer relay his messages. We had a strong alliance with the Vampire King, so his condolences were heartfelt and greatly appreciated. Nodding his approval and acceptance, Mason peered over to Vlad and raised his eyebrow.

Devlin, missing nothing, chuckled. "With protocol complete, may I introduce my outspoken companion?" Turning to the side with lightning fast reflexes, he reached out and slapped the back of the other vampire's head, causing him to grumble loudly.

"This fool is indeed called Vlad, but please don't hold that against him." Shaking his head, he laughed out loud, flashing a hint of fangs. "At our rebirth, we are given an opportunity to truly take on a new beginning by reinventing ourselves. Apparently, he believed the name Vlad gives him a touch of notoriety." Looking down, Devlin continued. "Me, I think it makes him sound foolish, but he is here solely in the role of an observer. He's still trying to find his place within our ranks, and I am his guardian. I apologize for his interruption, but the young one does have a point. If it wouldn't be too much of a hardship, Darcy, could you share your experience from last night?"

I knew this moment was coming and had prepared for it.

Mason leaned in and whispered, "You can do this, baby. Just share the facts and remember ... no guilt."

I nodded at his words and pushed myself back from my chair. On my feet, I looked around, meeting everyone's gaze.

Drawing in a deep steadying breath, I began going over everything—the trip to town, running into Gary, the gunshot, the change and hunting him down, then returning to find Mason and everyone by Jasmine's body. It seemed to pour out of me, and the more I spoke the easier it became.

I didn't need to see Mason to know he was beaming at me with pride. I paced as I shared the burden I'd been carrying and a tangle of emotions filled the air. There was so much of it, and when I was finished, I realized tears were not only steaming down my cheeks, but down several others as well. It was gut wrenching to share the horror and uncertainty, but I also felt stronger. I had been so worried of being judged and found unworthy, but all I could see was love and compassion.

Walking back to my seat, I entered into the embrace of Mason and stood there, soaking up his strength as he stroked my back tenderly. Tears flowed, but they were different this time. In voicing the events again, I realized I'd done my best, and although it didn't lessen my grief, it did calm me.

"I'm so proud of you, Darcy." His hot breath brushed against my ear before Mason kissed my forehead and helped me sit down. Standing tall, before leaning forward to brace himself on the table, he looked every inch the Alpha.

"Questions? Concerns?" he asked.

It was hard to breathe, and I think others felt it too because the room went deathly still.

It was Daniel who finally broke the silence. "I think I speak for everyone here, Darcy, by saying how proud we are, and just how much we love you. You'll find no condemnation from us." He looked around and each person nodded in agreement.

Gasping, I choked back a sob. There it was—acceptance, and a tremendous weight lifted from my shoulders. I covered my mouth with my hands, trying to rein myself in before I became a blubbering mess in front of everyone. Tears filled my eyes again, and all I could do was smile in gratitude.

Mason also relaxed, his muscular frame having tensed while waiting. As Alpha, his word was law, but he knew how much this meant to me. He clapped his hand on Daniel's back, as a form of thanks, before taking his seat again.

"What happened to what was left of Gary's body?"

Scanning the room, I noticed it was Jonas who spoke up.

"I personally took care of it as soon as I heard," Devlin responded, and was rewarded with another round of murmurs. "I know the Pack takes care of their own business, but I felt under the circumstances, it was the least I could do. I made sure no evidence was left behind at the scene, and have other Enforcers working on erasing Gary from any human system. Give it a few more hours and it will be as if he never existed."

"What arrangements have been made for Jasmine?" Daniel asked almost reverently.

Mason spoke up this time and I was curious as well. I wasn't sure whether any plans had been made, seeing he spent the last few hours with me. Guilt began to creep in again over taking so much of his time, but as his hand slid over to my thigh, the slight pressure was reminder enough. Being together had been important—needful. I placed mine over his and squeezed.

"Some of her pack sisters are with her at the moment, preparing her for the farewell ritual. We'll be holding it tonight after sunset. Vivien has agreed to officiate and does us a great honor by doing so."

A warm rush of emotion filled my body. This wasn't something the witch did often, but it was fitting. As the Alpha's sister, Jasmine would have the perfect send off, and I recognized the significance of the gesture. Vivien was also showing her support of the Mystic Wolves.

Mason moved on to next part of business. "I'm assuming Zane is interested in how vampire blood comes into play with last night." Devlin nodded as the Alpha continued. "From what Darcy's shared, it gave

Gary extra strength and a crazed appearance—made him unreachable to logic and her attempts to talk him down."

I'm sure I wasn't the only one curious about how he obtained the blood and for what purpose.

Devlin interrupted my thoughts with his comments. "The blood would have heightened everything—brain and physical functions, emotions and rationality. Depending on how long he was using, he would've been highly unstable—his actions proving so."

There it was in all its ugliness. Blood addict ... user. But why? From what I knew of Gary, there was no need for such measures. He never showed any interest in Jasmine before now, and always appeared to be a happy, well-adjusted human who appreciated the friendship of the pack. It made the drama of the past twenty-four hours even more disturbing. It was completely out of character.

"Has anyone else seen him use while he was here? Seen him act differently?" Jonas asked.

No one had.

"No offense, but why the hell do we care?" Eric spoke up. "The human was a traitor. He's been around us all enough to know not to mess with things he didn't understand. If he was in some kind of trouble, he could've come to any one of us and we would've stepped in. He was a coward, and I don't see why we need to waste any more time talking about the why of the situation. All we need to know is where he got it from and let the Enforcers do their job."

I turned to Mason for his reaction, watching him reflect on what was being said. He took a moment or two before he spoke again, with a very clear, authoritative tone.

"We care because I'll be damned if this happens again. Not just to us, but anyone. I know it's not pack business to be involved in the distribution of vampire blood, but I didn't bring this to our doorstep. Gary did. We won't stop until we find out and put an end to this. No one should have to bury family members and loved ones. Not like this." Facing Devlin, Mason continued. "What do you need from me?"

"Not much. I have a team going through Gary's things at his home, trying to find clues before they remove everything. They're checking past calls, asking neighbors before they scrub memories. I'm not sure how much we'll learn, but whatever we do I'll share with you. You might need to prepare yourself for the chance there's nothing to discover."

Mason bowed his head, stewing on the thought when a cell phone rang, bringing everyone's attention to Vlad. Releasing a growl, he leaned forward, causing the young vampire to shrug apologetically while trying to turn off the annoying sounds of his ringtone, Kung Fu Fighting.

"Did no one warn you what happens to cell phones in Pack meetings?"

I tried not to giggle as Mason laid the intimidation on thick. Daniel didn't even try to bother as he let out a loud bellow.

"My Lord of Beasts, you'll make him faint if you don't stop with the growling!"

Mason groaned at the title his second-in-command used. A quick glance told me Daniel wasn't far off. Vlad was white as a sheet, and his hand holding the phone trembled.

"Excuse yourself, young one, before the Alpha decides to eat you." Devlin chuckled. This caused the vampire to blanch further before leaving the room at an almost dead run. The Enforcer shook his head, finding the situation entertaining. "Did you really need to do that, Mason? Terrifying him is my responsibility."

"I know, but I couldn't resist. I thought the moment needed a little humor. Wanted to make my Darcy smile." Mason took hold of my hand and raised it to his mouth, kissing the back of it. Heat spread across my cheeks as I felt myself blush, and the room filled with soft laughter. Everyone was used to seeing their Alpha openly show his affections.

"Is there anything else we need to discuss, or are we good?" someone asked.

Without taking his eyes off me, Mason nodded, and the sound of chairs being pushed back echoed. He released my hand and added, "Make sure you stay available. If I need you, I'll let you know. See you all tonight."

The door burst opened and Vlad re-entered, screeching a panicked filled, "Wait!"

Devlin snorted. "Please. Must you be so dramatic? What is so important you need to rush in here like a hysterical woman?"

Before I could add my indignation, he looked at me and winked. "Present company excluded," he said as I stuck my tongue out at him. He rewarded with a warm smile. As instantly as it flashed, Devlin shut everything back down and turned back to his companion. "Spit it out, Vlad. Don't keep us waiting."

The young vampire's mouth flapped open two or three times as his eyes darted around the room. It was obvious he was reluctant to share the news which confused me. Didn't he just come in here and tell us to wait? Judging from the annoyed looks of my pack brothers, they were also wondering the same thing. Now wasn't the time for games.

"Oh for heaven's sake, tell us whatever it is before I let the wolves tear into you."

Vlad looked around frightened and Daniel didn't help matters by growling, flashing sharp fangs.

Shaking my head, I interjected. "Please, Vlad. Don't mind everyone. It looks like you have something to share." I tried to lace my voice with soothing tones, and I noticed him relax somewhat.

That peace was shattered, however, by Devlin grabbing the young man by the scruff of the neck and pushing him down into a chair. "Speak. Now."

Taking a hesitant breath, Vlad gestured to the empty seats and whispered. "You all might want to retake your places. I just received a message I think bears importance."

Heavy sighs and frustrated mutters covered the air. One comment sounded very close to a threat should the "fang-boy" be wasting time. A murmured assent followed with the loud sound of cracking knuckles.

Now with the room's attention solely on him, Vlad had very little to say and needed a reminding tap from Devlin to prompt him. Even my head hurt as I watched, and I lifted my hand to rub away the sympathy pain.

"There was a message delivered in the last thirty minutes to the King." He stopped, looking expectantly around the room as if it was meant to explain everything.

"You're trying my patience, youngling. Speak what you know, or I'll rip it from your throat. Regardless of who you are." The threat lay heavy in Devlin's voice. "What was the message?"

"A dead body—well at least what looks like one. According to those who were there, it more resembled a mass of raw, bloodied, meat. The sentries were making the hourly sweep, found it outside the gates to the estate, and raised the alarm. Reports say the blood amount was so incredible it took vast strength to resist partaking. On further inspection, it looks as though it was a human woman."

If Vlad didn't already look agitated, he did now as he continued. "Inspecting the surroundings, they found two items they felt the Alpha needed to know, and if I'm permitted to suggest, may be connected to what happened last night." The young vampire had our complete attention.

Mason was the next to speak, his confusion breaking the silence. "What were the objects, and why would they think I would need to be informed. Is it connected to Gary?"

Vlad lifted his cell phone and began touching the screen, searching for something before passing the device toward the Alpha.

"They forwarded me three images and asked if you knew what they meant." The phone made its way into Mason's hand, and I shifted in my seat so I could look with him. When he pushed the screen, illuminating it, I couldn't help my gasp of horror.

There was so much blood. I prayed that it had been quick and whoever it was hadn't suffered, because the violence it would've taken to accomplish the scene left me speechless.

Mason was tightlipped, and I felt him thrum with energy beside me. His wolf was stirring. I was sure of it because the air suddenly crackled with electricity, eliciting a round of growls from the rest of the pack in response. The Alpha was unsettled and it didn't bode well.

With the scroll of his thumb, he moved on to the next image—a piece of paper with some words scribbled on it.

I peered in closer, but I didn't need to as Mason

read it.

"How many women must die before you lose everyone you love?" He flipped back to the previous photo, but it was just as indiscernible as before. He looked back at the note, and started to speak, but Vlad interrupted.

"It was written in blood, and before you ask, look at the last image."

Now I was confused as a bloodied driver's license filled the screen. The owner was a pretty young woman, but someone I wasn't familiar with. I raised my head to ask Mason whether he knew her, and was rewarded with a not-so-subtle cuss. Seems he did, and judging by the fury that flashed in his eyes, she meant something to him.

Dropping the phone, he pushed back the seat and began pacing, raking his fingers through his hair. One of the greatest things about Mason was he usually had a cool head under pressure, and he made a point not to become unhinged in front of others. I was stunned by how truly rattled he was, and I could almost taste his impending change on my tongue. He needed to settle before he forced a shift on everyone.

My own wolf raised her head and howled, feeling the energy being generated, and I struggled to coax her back to sleep. I glanced around at the others, and they were also trying to rein themselves in. If something didn't happen, Devlin and Vlad would soon find themselves in a room full of wolves.

"What is it, Mason? Who is she?" I placed my hand on his arm as he brushed by, bringing him to a halt. Breathe. I sent the thought through our connection and was relieved when he took a deep lungful of air.

Steadying himself, he finally realized what effect his reaction was having on everyone, and a wave of calmness flowed through the room.

Retaking his chair, composed and back in charge of his emotions, Mason began to answer my questions. "Her name is ...," he paused, "was Vanessa Madison. She was a childhood sweetheart of mine, and playmate to Jasmine. Her father was a work colleague of my father, so our families would spend some time together. I haven't seen her in maybe ... three or four years. Last time I checked, she was finishing up with grad school and getting ready to move across the country."

"Who have you pissed off, Mason?" Daniel responded. "I think fang boy over there is right. It's too coincidental. Someone's trying to get your attention and will go to any lengths."

"Well, whoever it is has a death wish coming after the Alpha. I say we hunt them down and ...."

Wade was interrupted by Mason. "Let's settle down. Look over everything. Devlin, will you be able to stay longer?"

A nod from the Enforcer was all that was needed.

Facing the group, the Alpha continued. "Eric, put everyone on high alert. Send for members to come in and set up a team to begin perimeter surveillance. Nothing in, nothing out until we know more." Finally, he turned his focus to me.

"I know. No going anywhere. Stay at the house, and no traipsing in the woods."

"Just until we know what's going on, okay? Promise me." His gaze held mine.

"Girl Scouts honor," I replied, raising my hand to salute.

"You weren't even a girl scout, Darcy." Mason chuckled, and his smile almost reached his eyes. He caressed the side of my face with his fingers. "Safety first. I can't lose you too."

I nodded, as I briefly leaned into his touch. When he broke the contact, I refocused on the room and stood. "Well, I'll leave everyone to figure this out." I pushed my chair under the table, and Mason reached out to grab hold of my hand.

"Where can I find you when this is finished?" He studied my face as if he was afraid this was the last time he'd see me.

"I have a ritual to help prepare. And goodbyes to offer." Letting my fingers trail out of his grasp, I nodded to those in the room, pausing a moment to touch Devlin's shoulder. "Thanks for being here." He squeezed my hand and I exited quickly, closing the door on the meeting turned war council.

What a change of events. Shaking my head, I began my journey toward Jasmine's room, my heart preparing itself for the next few hours.

Chapter Twelve

It was into a quiet hush—a reverent silence—when I slipped inside Jasmine's room, closing the door softly behind me. The curtains had been drawn, candles lit on almost every surface, and it gave the space a solemn ambience befitting the moment.

Not ready to look at the bed where my beloved friend and pack sister lay, I gazed around the place I'd spent so many hours in. Echoes of memories flittered about in my mind, and it tugged on my heart strings because I truly, and deeply, loved Jasmine.

Our connection had been almost instant, two hearts reaching out, and rejoicing in finding one another. Similar in age and tastes, our friendship had steadily grown until we became inseparable—in thoughts and actions. Mason would laugh so hard each time we finished each other's sentences, and would groan over the antics we'd get up to.

He always shared how good it felt knowing we were close, easing a burden I never knew he carried. He worried over his sister, afraid she'd be lonely if his future mate didn't recognize the importance Jasmine held in his life.

Back in the room, something pulled me toward the bookshelf which was crammed—filled with some of Jasmine's favorite reads. It was the photo frame I'd given her for her last birthday—a silver one with the words "best friends" stamped into it. I gingerly picked it up, my eyes never leaving the smiling faces peering back up at me. I traced her image, marveling at the glow the camera had been able to capture.

I couldn't even remember when we took the picture, we'd taken so many. Judging from the goofy looks, I'd say it was from one of the many nights we used to lie giggling on top of her bed together, taking random poses. No matter the occasion, we always found some reason to be silly, and would spend hours trying to outdo the last shot.

Both our mouths were open, teeth sparkling, but the twinkle in our eyes showed it all. We were best friends. We were happy, and we had the rest of our lives ahead of us.

It hurt my heart knowing the last part wasn't true anymore. Placing the frame back on the shelf, I began randomly pulling out books. It was another thing Jasmine and I had in common—our love of reading romance, and the sexy heroes we found in each story. I couldn't count how many times we would text, or show up at each other's rooms, gushing over what Mr. McSwoony was doing, and sighing together. We were complete junkies, and would stay up all night talking about what it would be like to be transported into one of the books. We had weaknesses for highlanders, and no matter how hard we tried, we could never get Mason to speak in a Scottish brogue.

I laughed out loud, remembering how we used to badger him.

"Please, Mason ... just say it. Just once, and we'll go away."

"No, Jasmine. Now leave me alone."

"Not even for me?" Running my finger down his chest, I bat my eyelashes at him. If anyone could get him to cave, it was me. I was his weakness after all.

"Not you too! Enough, I'm not going to speak like your silly romance books." Mason backed up, a frown on his face as he struggled to look serious. "How will people respect me as Alpha if they know I gave into your demands?"

"Awww, come on, Brother. It's not like we're asking you to wear a kilt and swing around a sword. Just a few words—for us. Pleeeeassee." Jasmine wasn't beyond begging.

"Hmmm, a kilt. I think that's even better. Forget the words. Wear a plaid for us. Show us that fine body of yours!" I began to move toward him, a wicked grin covering my face.

He fled after that, spending the rest of the afternoon hiding in his office. Jasmine and I returned to her room and laughed for hours, devising plans on how we could convince him.

Leaving the bookshelf, I noticed I wasn't alone in the room. April was curled up on the chair, head resting on her hands as she slept against the seat arm. New to the pack by a year, she was also the youngest and looked up to Jasmine a lot. It made sense if anyone would be keeping vigil, it would be her.

Shaking her shoulder gently, I whispered for her to wake up. Recognition was slow as she opened her sleepy eyes and they instantly filled with tears.

"Hi, Darcy. I'm sorry I fell asleep. I didn't mean to." She stretched her small frame and yawned.

"How long have you been here?"

"Since Mason and everyone brought her in. A few of the pack sisters helped get her situated, cleaned up and changed her clothes before they all left." She looked at the floor, speaking softly. "I didn't think she'd want to be left alone so I stayed."

The thoughtfulness of April struck me hard, and I offered her a grateful smile. Even though we didn't always pull her into our circle, she loved Jasmine enough to know her well.

"You're right. Jasmine wouldn't have liked that. Thank you for being here." I reached out, and April moved into my open arms. As we stood there embracing, she let out a flood gate of cries, the depth of her grief filling the small room. Stroking her back gently, I vowed to keep a closer eye on her, making sure she knew I was always there.

"Did you come to sit with her?" The question was quickly followed by a hiccup. Using the back of her hand, April made a quick job at mopping up her tears. My heart broke for her—broke for all of us.

"I did, so why don't you head back to your bedroom for a while, and try to get some sleep. Your bed would be more comfortable than the chair." Gently leading her to the door, she seemed a little hesitant to leave. "The Alpha has shared the farewell ritual will be tonight at sunset. I'll make sure someone comes to get you, okay?"

Turning around with a serious expression on her face, April added softly, "If you have to leave and no-one is around, come get me."

Promising her I would, I went back inside with Jasmine, alone for the first time since this nightmare began. I fidgeted with my clothing, my fingers desperate to be moving. I took a step towards the bed, and faltered. I didn't think I was strong enough for this. Everything in me screamed to turn and walk away, not to look—not to face the truth.

My wolf raised her head and gently bayed, a soft serenade of comfort. I felt her brush against me, and a feeling of peace flowed through me. She was lending me strength—strength I didn't have on my own. Sighing deeply, I closed my eyes and reminded myself I would survive this. I approached the bed and the piece of my heart that lay there, forever sleeping.

She was beautiful. Even in death, Jasmine stole my breath, so peaceful ... so still ... so young.

If I didn't know the truth, I would've sworn until I was blue in the face she was sleeping. Her facial features were relaxed and a slight smile rested on her lips. I couldn't see any of the horror from before, someone having erased the evidence. Whoever it had been, I would be forever grateful because I knew Jasmine's last moments weren't happy—far from it.

Not caring to hide the trembling in my hand, I brushed my fingers through her fine blonde hair, combing it a little over the pillow. She always thought a woman's hair was their crowning glory and she was always so meticulous with it. I was the kind to dry and put in a ponytail, but Jasmine ... she could spend forever brushing, straightening, or curling it. I would lie on her bed and tease her relentlessly over it, but she just smiled and told me to shush.

Dragging one of the seats over to her bed side to sit, I released the breath I'd been holding. Step one accomplished and I was still okay. I looked down the length of the bed. Someone had clothed her in her favorite dress and lightly covered her with a blanket, as if protecting her from the cold. It was a thoughtful gesture.

I glanced over her body, as if trying to check she was all there and accounted for. I knew I was being silly, but still I did it, almost like how Mason had done it with me—two arms, two legs, and a body. She was in one piece, sleeping. I caught the lie and didn't bother correcting myself.

I reclined in my chair, and exhaled heavily.

"Oh, Jasmine." The words hung in the air, suspended by a hope I knew I shouldn't have.

Abruptly leaning forward, I raised my voice. "Wake up, girlfriend. Time to rise and shine. Who said you could be lazy and sleep all day?" I peered at her, waiting for her to open her eyes and poke her tongue at me.

Nothing.

"You're missing out on things. Daniel's driving Mason crazy by calling him all kinds of titles. Sooner or later, your brother is going to pound on him. Who'll be there bandage the fool if you're not awake to help?" Grasping at straws, I used her crush on Daniel to try to coax her back.

My beautiful sister continued to lay still.

Without thinking, I reached out and took hold of her hand, squeezing it. The instant I touched her, I realized my mistake. Grief beat down on me with such force that a sob erupted out of my mouth and I whipped my arm back, shaking my head frantically.

"No. No. No." Somewhere in my mind, I kept telling myself if I denied the truth, I could keep pretending. But the proof was in the chill over her skin, the stiffness of death, and it shattered me.

It didn't matter I'd been surrounded by violence all my life. The reality of death wasn't something new, especially being part of the supernatural community, because there was always something happening, some feud—particularly amongst the packs. This felt different though. It struck too deep because this had been personal—my relationship with Jasmine a strong one.

Pulling my legs up into my chest, I wrapped my arms around my knees and cried. She truly was gone and nothing was bringing her back.

The room felt confining—like the air had been sucked from it, and I struggled to catch my breath. I refused to open my eyes, not ready to see again what my heart was not accepting as fact. We had spoken about it. I had remembered the events and thought I acknowledged it. But this—her cold hand—was like a slap in the face ... a proverbial kick in the gut.

Are you okay?

Mason. He'd reached out through our connection and I could imagine him, face concerned, ready to finish what he was doing so he could come. I shook my head, even though I knew he couldn't see me do it. He was needed where he was. There were other things of importance. He had already helped me over the worst and this too would pass.

I am. How are you doing? Meeting almost over? I hoped we'd be able to get a few moments alone together before the ritual, just so I could make sure he'd at least eaten something today. I knew he'd been on the go and he had to be exhausted.

I could almost feel his sigh as he answered. I'm doing okay. It's been a long day, so once I'm done here, I'll come get you.

The connection closed and I spent the next few moments soaking in the surrounding silence. I sat there in the glow of the flickering candlelight until I found myself speaking out loud again.

"I'm sorry, Jasmine." I remained quiet as I let my apology settle. "But I got justice. I wasn't able to protect you, or stop it from happening, but I did avenge you. That has to mean something, doesn't it?" My voice was small, almost childlike in tone.

Looking over at my best friend, suddenly there didn't seem enough time to tell her everything my heart contained. All those unspoken moments and thoughts were begging to be released. How many times did I say, "Oh, I'll tell her tomorrow," or, "I'll wait until I see her next?" Staring at her, I realized there would be no more tomorrows for us. I did something I didn't think I would've had the strength for only moments earlier.

Careful not to disturb her, I inched myself toward her, lowering my body down beside her on the bed. Ignoring the cold feel, I took hold of her hand and began from the start. I poured out my heart and shared everything, no matter how small, or insignificant. Whatever entered my mind, I shared and soon all my hopes, dreams, and memories filled the room.

It was our final bantering session—our last time staring at the ceiling while baring our souls. I held onto the hope and belief that wherever Jasmine was, she was listening and smiling. She was at peace and missing me just as much as I was her.

A blanket of exhaustion fell over me, making my words jumble as I fought yawn after yawn. Soon it became difficult to speak, as I settled deeper into the bed, and with one final whisper, I gave in to sleep.

"Goodbye Jasmine. I love you."

Chapter Thirteen

Something was stroking my face, leaving trails of tingles in its path as it grazed over my cheek before moving toward my jawline. I groaned, the sensation causing my skin to flush and break out into goose bumps. I stretched out lazily before remembering where I was.

My eyes opened quickly, terrified of what might be touching me, and I squeaked in shock when I found a pair of beautiful blue eyes staring back. I should've known it was Mason.

Cautiously propping up, expecting to find myself still in Jasmine's room, the familiarity of my own greeted me, and I realized what must have happened. He found me and had carried me back to my own bed to continue sleeping. Reclining back again, I snuggled into his body to enjoy the contact.

I loved moments like this where we didn't have to speak, but could find comfort and warmth from lying beside each other.

"Good afternoon, sleepy head." His voice never ceased to give me goose bumps. He spoke in low tones that rumbled a little, and I loved how sexy it made him sound. Sometimes I wondered if he did it on purpose, just to make me smile.

"I guess the meeting is over and you found me, huh?" I smoothed down the front of his t-shirt, enjoying the way his muscles moved underneath.

"Yeah, I figured I knew where you were and you looked so peaceful so I just brought you back here instead of waking you. You've been out for a good hour or two so you needed it." Resting on his back, Mason turned his head to kiss me on top of mine before staring at the ceiling. "What a day."

I nodded and we lay there in silence, with him stroking the side of my arm and me tracing the contours of his stomach. We were lost in thought—not wanting to spoil how we were feeling with the ugliness of events.

Releasing a tired sigh, Mason spoke first. "It goes without saying you're not to leave the house, right? No trips to town, not so much as a toe off pack property." I knew he was trying to sound casual, but I could sense the importance hidden in his voice. This would be something I couldn't argue about. He was on alert and the conditions of my safety were non-negotiable.

"I promise. Stay at home. Be a good girl. Don't cause trouble." I rattled off each sentence like I was reading a grocery list.

He laughed at my last comment. "I don't think it's feasible for you to keep out of mischief, but at least try to keep it within the estate. I can't expect the impossible from you. Trouble is your middle name after all."

I slapped him for that, the sound of my hand thudding against his chest echoed in the room, and was followed quickly by a flare of pain in my palm. It was like hitting a brick wall.

"You doing okay?" Instinctively, I knew he was asking if I was alright after sitting with Jasmine. I couldn't help but smile at just how thoughtful he was. Even though we'd been together for a while, I still wasn't accustomed to how in tune he was with me, how he noticed things and genuinely wanted to help. The jerks I dated in the past couldn't have cared less. Their one focus was how soon they could get in my pants and get out.

I hugged Mason tightly, trying to convey how much I appreciated him before letting out a huge sigh. "I'm good. I just kept telling myself I can survive this, and even though it hurts, I still have you and she wouldn't want me falling apart—especially not now with everything happening. It still feels like I have a lump in my throat all the time, like something's missing, but I know she would want me to continue to live. It was just a shock seeing her—touching her. It made it real and my mind couldn't refuse it." I blew a strand of hair out of my eyes and smiled when Mason reached over to tuck it behind my ear. "I'm glad I was able to have those last moments with her. We talked. Well, I talked and she listened."

"So it was like normal." His fingers began to slowly run through my hair, twirling it in a soothing fashion. "I can't tell you how many times I passed her door and heard you both in there laughing away, not knowing what you two were up to, but so glad you had each other. As a brother, it meant a lot that you both got on so well. It felt right."

More silence followed as we both got lost in our thoughts. Sunshine blazed through the window, heating the air, and for that short period of time, everything felt perfect. It wouldn't be difficult to convince myself this was just an ordinary afternoon and everything was right in the world. I lifted my hand into the ray of light that covered most of Mason's upper body.

Turning it back and forth, rubbing my fingers together, it amazed me how easy it is to take for granted the simple things. I'd grown so accustomed to seeing things every day, always assuming they'd be there whenever I needed them. All it took was an instant to lose it and it would be gone forever. Staring at the dust particles dancing in the sun beam, I vowed to never become so complacent again and learn to appreciate everything I had.

"Those are some heavy thoughts there, Darcy," Mason's voice jarred me from my musings.

"Reading my mind, are we?" I poked his ribs with my finger and was rewarded with a squirm. I loved how he was ticklish.

"No, but this huge frown wrinkle gave you away." He traced my brow and I slapped him hard.

"You did not just tell me I have wrinkles, Mason O'Connor. These are not things women like to hear from the men who love them. You're not supposed to see our imperfections!" I covered my forehead with my hand, trying to hide any visible flaws.

He gently pried my arm down, kissing my palm before placing it on his chest, over his heart. "I don't see imperfections, sweetheart. All I've ever seen is you and you've always dazzled me."

"Smooth answer. I think I'll let you live for a few more hours." I laughed and I tilted my head back to kiss his chin. Thinking better of it, I nipped the skin lightly with my teeth, letting my tongue flicker over the spot. Contented, I rested back into him. I could sense the moment when he became serious by the way his body tensed, and the feel of the air became a little thicker.

"I can't promise this won't get messy. I'm not sure who's behind the message, or how it includes Gary and Jasmine, but something in my gut tells me this is going to get bad. If there's one thing I've learned is to always trust my instincts, the edge I have as Alpha, and right now, it's screaming danger. I need to know whatever happens you're going to be safe. No matter what." He slid his arm out from under me so he could prop himself up. As he peered down at me, I reached up to trace his brow.

"Now who has wrinkles?"

"I'm serious, Darcy. I can't give my entire focus if I'm worried about you ignoring orders."

"Are you ordering me?" I raised my eyebrow.

"In this? Yes. As Alpha and your future mate, I'm ordering you stay on the property." He looked so solemn and I felt the weight of his command rest on me. Even if I wanted to disobey, I couldn't.

"I love you." I smiled up at him, those three words letting him know I'd heard and would follow. Last night scared me, and no amount of independence was worth a repeat. "Now can you finally kiss me?"

My insides quivered as I watched the slow progression of a heart stopping grin cross his face and the way his eyes turned to instant smolder. I licked my lips in anticipation, slightly breathless as I waited for him to lower his head and press his lips against mine.

"What is it about you that I can't resist?" he asked, inching painstakingly lower until he hovered just about my mouth, barely touching. His breath was hot, seductive, and it caused a ripple of excitement to course through me.

"Must be my sparkling personality," I whispered back, struggling not to close the distance between us. Electricity charged the air, the chemistry of our connection wreaking havoc on my hormones.

He feathered his lips lightly over mine, just the ghost of a touch and I whimpered as he retreated without fully claiming my mouth. "Must be because I can barely remember my name when you look at me like that." His fingers drew a soft line down the side of my cheek.

"And how is that?" I purred softly, a sultry tone to my voice. My body felt as if it would explode from the way he seemed to drink me in.

"Like the world doesn't exist, but for the two of us. How did I deserve you?" He kissed me again. This time a little slower, pressing harder, and I followed him involuntarily as he moved back. He was teasing me and driving me crazy with it.

"You talk too much, Mason."

Done with being tormented with waiting, I grabbed hold of the back of his head and crushed his mouth down onto mine. I didn't wait for an invitation, my tongue eagerly twining with his and I groaned as his taste filled me.

As quickly as passion ignited, I reined myself in, slowing the tempo of our kiss and turning it into the languid kind of touch we both reveled in. I loved it because it felt like it shattered me from the inside out, liquefying my bones and leaving me breathless all at the same time.

It was impossible not to move, the pull of the moment acting like a magnet as our bodies fell into perfect alignment. Hands gently teased, causing moans of pleasure, and when it was time to break apart, I tugged on his lower lip, reluctant to let go. I sucked it into my mouth, tracing it with my tongue before fully releasing him, a contented sigh bubbling out from me.

"Can we just stay like this forever?" I couldn't think of a better way to spend the day.

"You like kissing me, huh?"

I snorted. I couldn't help it. Of all the crazy things I'd ever heard him say, this was too much. I followed my unladylike response with a roll of my eyes and a shrug of my shoulders. "It's okay, I guess. It wasn't completely horrible."

I was rewarded for my blatant lie by a round of relentless tickling, Mason showing no mercy as I screamed and begged for him to stop. It drove me nuts he knew my weaknesses, the certain parts of my body which responded wildly to the right touch.

"Just as well I think your kisses are kind of okay too. Who knows what would become of us if we couldn't tolerate each other." He crossed his eyes and stuck his tongue out the side of his mouth, pulling a face before adding, "Complete torture if you ask me."

"You liar! My kisses are divine. You live for every single one I give you, and I know they make your knees a little weak. Admit it!" I laughed out loud, scolding him.

"Baby, that's something you girls do. Men don't get weak kneed or whatever dramatic term you want to use. We're manly. We kiss and dominate, leaving our prey defenseless to our advances." He leaned in and kissed me. Not a deep, soulful one, but definitely enough that when he leaned back, I was wearing a goofy smile.

His hand grabbed hold of my leg, fondling it, and a look of triumph blazed from his face. "See, just as I expected. Your knees are weak."

"You're such a dork, Mason. But you're mine, so that's okay." I fingered the locks of hair that curled behind his ears. "You need a haircut." I started to brush the strands out, moving across the rest of his head, measuring in my mind how much would need to go.

"We're lying here together, talking about kissing, and you're focused on my hair? There's something wrong with this picture, babe. Drastically wrong."

"Well, do something about it then ...," I lowered my voice to a gentle hush. "Mr. Big, Bad Wolf." I grinned back at him and winked.

His eyes flared, the wolf surfacing briefly to answer the call before he offered a wicked smile that threatened to scorch my insides. "That sounded very much like a dare. Sure you want to go there?"

"Oh, I very much want to go there. If you think you have what it takes, then step up to the plate and show me what you've got." I winked before adding, "That's unless you think you're not capable."

Brat, was the only word I heard before he seized my mouth completely, setting me on fire with the mastery of his touch. Heat built up, whipping around us as his tongue repeatedly swirled and plunged in my mouth. Mason answered my taunts with a kiss so spectacular, I thought my body would lift off the bed and float away.

He was relentless, methodical in his ministrations, easing up to let me catch my breath before sinking me back under and stealing it again. My entire being focused solely on him and the exquisite feeling pulsating through me.

I didn't flinch as his hand tugged on my shirt, pulling it free from my jeans. Neither did I pause when I felt his warm fingers rest on my rib cage. His touch excited me, the way it caused me to tingle, and he absolutely turned my world upside down.

Arching my back, I pressed my skin into his palm so wherever he had contact branded me. I didn't know where to focus on—my mouth or my body. Everything about him was unraveling me, one blinding stroke at a time.

I felt myself being lifted, so unaware of my surroundings, and I almost toppled when I found myself placed on my feet. Saving me from face planting onto my bed, Mason chuckled, scooping me up in his arms.

"Just as I expected, you can't even stand. I win the challenge."

I tried to tell him not to gloat, that it wasn't becoming, but all I could do was laugh, completely dazed and bewitched. He had literally kissed me senseless.

Watching Mason pause, he tilted his head to the side as if listening, and I knew something was happening. To some it may seem strange, but I'd seen him receive messages through the pack connection enough to know someone needed the Alpha.

"Duty calls?" I asked, finally able to find my voice. Slowly, I was beginning to focus on my surroundings, the effect of his kiss fading. All but the burn, which I knew would take a little longer to extinguish.

"Yeah. I need to go check something out, but before I do ...," he stopped talking and left the room, entering the adjoining bathroom. I heard things being moved around, bottles being picked up and placed back before the sound of water filling in the bathtub reached me. A few moments later he returned, a man on a mission, and lifted me into his arms.

"A new command from your Alpha." He winked at me as he set me on my feet in the bathroom. Without waiting, he began to undress me before placing me in the soothing hot water. A quick smell told me he added bath salts—lavender and eucalyptus—my favorite.

"Try to relax from now until I come and get you for Jasmine's farewell. Just lie here and soak in the tub. Dream about all the kisses I've yet to give you and nothing else. I'll be back in about an hour or so."

"But I just had a shower!" I laughed, staring up at him.

"That was for cleaning, this is for relaxing so quit complaining." He glanced around, looking as though he'd forgotten something. He hurried out of the room before returning with the paperback novel I'd left resting on the bedside table. "In case, you feel like reading." He winked.

I went to say something, but he leaned forward, not caring about the water that sloshed up and wet him as he kissed me quickly on the lips. "I love you."

Smiling, I closed my eyes, moaning about how good my muscles were beginning to feel. This wasn't about me getting clean, my shower earlier having taken care of it. I let my body relax, and softly hummed a random tune to myself.

This kind of pampering could be easy to get used to. I lifted my hand out of the water, watching the way it trickled down and the noise it made as it splashed.

"Go be the Alpha, Mason. I'll be here when you get back." I waved lazily, the effects of the lavender already lulling me into a contented state. "If you get back in time and the water is still warm enough, maybe you can join me."

It was hard to miss the flare of desire as he contemplated the idea. "Count on it." Leaving the room, hearing the door close behind him, I slid down in the tub, fully immersing myself.

This felt like heaven.

Chapter Fourteen

The evening's breeze felt good against my warm skin. Standing on the edge of the garden's perimeter, I took a moment to take in everything and let out a sigh. With my hand securely grasped in his, I felt the gentle tug of Mason pulling me forward.

Whoever prepared the outside had done a phenomenal job, one worthy to be a tribute for a beloved pack sister and friend. With the sun having finally set and the chirp of cicadas filling the air, it was the perfect night, and I sent an upward thanks to the gods. I didn't want anything to tarnish the ritual, this being the final show of respect from the Pack.

The lawn was aglow with what seemed like countless lanterns, candles aflame that cast delicate shadows upon the ground. It set an almost ethereal mood on those already in attendance, everyone speaking in reverent tones as they huddled together in small, intimate groups.

A hush came over everyone as they noticed us pass through. Hands reached out in comfort and condolences, some breaking away from others to speak brief words of solace. Jasmine's death had shaken us as a whole. I could see it reflected in everyone's faces and the tears already beginning to flow.

There wasn't just pack members here, others from the supernatural community had come to pay their homage, and it showed the level of admiration and respect Mason had earned for them to be there.

Devlin stood closely by his King, Zane, and a quick glance found Vlad standing off to one side, looking awkward.

As we passed by Zane, Mason stopped and accepted the embrace he was pulled into. There was history between these two great leaders, and it was an affectionate one. The vampire king whispered something into the Alpha's ear, his hand resting firmly on his shoulder.

I walked into Devlin's arms, his body offering temporary comfort as he also murmured how truly sorry he was.

Moving to Mason's side, I missed the short conversation, but caught the end nod of agreement, and the brief pat on the back before we continued on to the front of the congregation. With chairs arranged in lines and an aisle down the center, Vivien faced us on the dais that had been erected. Wearing the ceremonial robes befitting her station as the lead witch, she looked elegant and deeply saddened.

I thought I had no more tears left as our eyes linked, and she inclined her head to the side as if reading me. Vivien was someone who I greatly admired, and I cherished the relationship we'd been able to foster. She was a wise confidante, someone with unfailing loyalty, and I could feel the calming energy she radiated into the crowd, as she stepped down and walked towards us.

Her arms opened for Mason. "Darling boy, I'm so sorry. This is something I couldn't have foreseen and would never have wished for you. To lose both parents, and now your sister, you are too young to have experienced such loss." I watched as the embrace ended, and she caressed the side of his face. "Please know I am here, should you ever need to talk. Your mother would've been so proud."

The comment seemed to make him stand a little taller, and I was grateful he'd been given that reminder. Even though his relationship with his father had been tenuous at best, he had been close to his mother and she would've loved to have seen the man he was.

Vivien continued to hold Mason's attention. "Remember, brave Alpha, this too shall pass, and before you know it, you'll be reunited with your beloved sister. Keep your focus on the future." I loved hearing the slight accent she had. I hastily brushed away my tears, and she turned to me. Using her finger to slant my face back, she gazed deeply into my eyes—looking, reading, studying.

Taking hold of both of our hands, she clasped them together, squeezing them with hers before releasing them. "Yes, you truly are the perfect match. You will both be fine and will rise above what is to come."

She nodded to herself, pleased, before turning her focus onto the crowd gathered. She really did give off a regal air, and I could see why so many people held her in high esteem. She was a revered leader and a formidable opponent. With the ritual soon to start, we walked alongside her back up on to the dais.

A feeling beckoned me, pulling my gaze away and I looked behind Vivien. I found myself staring at Jasmine lying on the makeshift altar. She was shrouded in the most exquisite sheer material, and she looked like something out of a fairytale.

She wore a simple shift of lavender, intricate beading on the bodice the only embellishment. Her hair was brushed out and arranged into braids, with small blossoms and ribbons threaded through. I noticed again how peaceful she looked, like a slumbering princess waiting for her prince to come and kiss her back to life. Surrounding her body were flowers of every kind, and the floral scent filled the air.

"She always was the beautiful one of the family."

My quiet musings were broken by the soft words of Mason.

"I used to tease her about all the broken hearts she'd leave in her wake. I guess she'll be doing that where she is now." He wore a gentle smile, but I saw the pain behind it.

"She loved her big brother," I replied, catching a stray tear with my finger.

Vivien came up behind us, motioning for us to take our seats and I mouthed to my future mate my belief we'd get through this.

Paying one last look at his treasured sibling, Mason led us down to the waiting chairs. I noticed April was sitting alone a few rows back and I motioned for her to join us before turning my gaze to the front.

Lifting her arms in a welcoming fashion, small balls of light seemed to appear out of nowhere and floated above us in the air. A reminder of the power she held, it also increased the beauty of the moment and signaled the beginning of the ritual. I couldn't help but gaze upwards and marvel at the magic involved as they faintly twinkled like mini fireflies dancing.

"I welcome you here tonight, esteemed family and friends of the Mystic Wolves pack. It's with troubled hearts we gather to say a goodbye to our dearest Jasmine, sister of the Alpha. But more importantly, we meet to celebrate the life of one who shone brightly in the short time she was amongst us."

A warm sensation settled over me like a sigh and I snuggled in closer to Mason. Fitting perfectly under his arm, I rested my hand on his thigh, and he placed his on top of mine. It seemed as though the world stopped, taking time from its constant orbit to witness the sacred rite. Everything subsided, all noise and commotion waning as if a powerful spell was being cast. We were pulled into its weave, its heady influence offering a peace greatly needed.

"Life doesn't always go as we expect it to. Even with the most marvelous of powers, we're helpless against what's written in the stars. Whether you believe in fate, or free will, there's always some kind of plan, some intricate design which governs over us and keeps the balance. Even when that balance is threatened, tearing us away from those we love, we must continue to trust there is a purpose, and hold on tightly to those who still walk with us."

"The humans have an interesting saying—there is a time and a season for everything. As supernatural beings, we also hold this belief true. Just as we rejoice in the blessings brought with each new life, we also mourn when one is extinguished. It's particularly hard when death comes beckoning early, or without reason, but I would share with you this—don't let grief weigh you down so much that you lose your way on the path. Feel what you will. Cry your tears, but always remember, even in the darkest of times there is hope. Remember those who have passed on and show your gratitude for them by continuing to live in a way that honors them. That way no life is ever wasted. Each life is revered and cherished."

"Jasmine was a precious soul, one blessed to be born into the werewolf legacy. We're each given unique traits, a heritage that ties us together as a community, and none are more fascinating than the lupus. The spirit of a human and wolf residing in the same vessel, a lifetime spent together as intimate companions. Each soul brings to the partnership strength and abilities, both seeking to find that perfect balance as they learn and accept one another. Our beloved sister and friend was at the beginning of her journey, her education only started, but already she had shown a great depth of character and compassionate heart. She and her wolf will be greatly missed, but never far away."

Having been to many funerals, this next part was always something that struck me deeply. It was the ritual of farewell where the body was consumed by witch's fire, releasing the spirits into the air so they could continue their journey into the afterlife together. There were many different tales about what happens next, each pack and group adding their own slant, so I was curious to see how Vivien spun her tale.

"The mythology of the werewolf is one buried deeply in lore, and as such, has many interpretations. Stories shared of centuries after retelling often add to the truth, but never forget—there is always beauty and honor at the center."

"My grandmother spoke of sitting at the knee of her mother and listening to the tale of the Lupus constellation." Lifting her arm up to the side, Vivien gestured to a group of stars sparkling in the night sky. "Formed in the shape of a wolf, it is said they stand there as punishment for the grievous sins performed against the Greek god, Zeus. Retaliating in anger, the father of all werewolves, Lycaon, was banished to the heavens, forever to watch over his descendants."

"Forever is a long time, an eternity of contemplation over the foolishness of pride—so my mother told me—and here is where my tale differs. After a millennia of observance, and having his heart filled with humility, Lycaon now stands as a constant sentinel. A reminder to others of the consequences of arrogance and hatred, an influence to countless generations seeking guidance, and the resting place for those who pass on."

"The farewell ritual is the forgiving practice, passed on by a benevolent god to help each descendent find their rest with their ancestors. Where once they were cursed to wander the earth, denied entrance to the afterlife because of the sins of one, the witch's fire was created to release and purify the dead, transporting them home."

A chill pulsed through me, and a reverent awe hovered over the crowd. I heard familiar snippets threaded through Vivien's heartfelt words, but this was by far the most profound retelling I'd experienced. Judging from the nodding of Mason's head, he too was feeling the same, and he raised our entwined hands to his mouth to place a kiss on the back. I felt a smaller hand grab hold of my other, and I turned to see the shy smile of April. She was just as affected, and I offered her a reassuring squeeze.

Moving about the dais now, positioning herself behind Jasmine, Vivien used a nearby lantern to light a taper. Holding the flame to a bundle of sage and prepared herbs, she began to waft the smoking leaves up the length of Jasmine's body. Chanting words too soft to hear, power began to build and rise, like the lulling of a wave, each one growing stronger and stronger into a swelling pitch.

The gentle breeze before us gradually picked up speed, raising the garments and hair of Vivien. The balls of light hovering in the air flared in intensity, but still she kept chanting, never losing focus. A different kind of electricity filled the air, one without the unique feel of Mason's Alpha energy.

Magic rippled and convulsed to the point where I began hearing the echo of gasps and exclamations behind me.

Suddenly, all the lights extinguished, plunging the garden into complete darkness. Even the moon seemed to hide its face, the stars fading to the point where the sky was like a black canvas—all but the Lupus constellation. Those stars shone brighter than anything I'd ever seen, as though they were alive and waiting.

A shimmer from the altar drew back my gaze and I let out an exalted sigh of surprise as I watched Jasmine's body instantly ignite with the most wondrous hues of purple and blue flame. Higher and higher the blaze flickered and burned, twisting and turning as though each spark was dancing.

A look of absolute love shone from Vivien's face as her hands began to move in intricate patterns, each gesture seemed effortless and filled with meaning. I couldn't pull my eyes away from the sight and caught myself leaning forward in the attempt to catch every nuance.

Tears streaked down each face, my own eyes blurring before I rapidly brushed mine away, so captivated we were as we seemed to hold our breaths for what we knew was coming. Even prepared, I gasped as I watched a beam of the purest white light break out of Jasmine's body, releasing two globes, which I knew were the spirits of the wolf and herself.

They seemed to glow and pulsate—one the prettiest of yellow and the other a deep forest green. I knew which one was Jasmine—the yellow, because I always felt she reminded me of the sun, life giving, a provider of warmth and always bestowing hope.

Gently, they drifted over the now empty vessel, twirling around each other as though they were excited in the newly found freedom they had. Fascinated, I watched the yellow globe, Jasmine, teeter towards us, almost hesitant, before floating over and frolicking between Mason and me. She was saying goodbye one last time. Letting us know she was happy and not to worry.

Mason stretched out his hand—palm up, and a cry erupted out of his tight frame as the delicate ball of spirit rested softly on his skin. A look of unadulterated reassurance crossed his face, his lips curling into a small smile before he nodded. Taking this as acceptance, Jasmine rejoined the green globe, and with one last dance around Vivien, they began to ascend up into the sky.

A familiar surge of energy pushed its way through the crowd as the Alpha issued the command to change. One by one, we stood and began, allowing our wolves to come forward and say their goodbyes.

I felt the solemn brush of my own wolf against my skin before she burst forth, bringing me to my hands and knees. All around me I could sense when each change was completed, Mason's happening almost instantly. With one accord, as a soulful tribute, I joined my pack and howled.

The night air was filled with the distinct bays and croons of a heartsick family who promised to never forget and to always be vigilant. The pledge to seek justice blended in amidst the voices, an oath to live each day as a way to honor someone most beloved. The music was hauntingly beautiful, and I joined my wolf by adding my love to her serenade.

Somewhere in the symphony, a lone voice emerged as though the heavens had opened and an angel had descended. The simplicity of the strand added to the harmony of our wolves, and it was as if the air threatened to explode. The world seemed to tilt, as if unprepared for such majesty, and looking around, I was stunned to find the source.

Devlin. My dearest friend Devlin, standing aside from everyone. Blood red tears streaming down his cheeks as he opened his mouth and offered his own sincere homage. Who would've known something so profound could've come from the Enforcer.

Casting my gaze back, the orbs of spirits slowly becoming too hard to distinguish as they rose into the heavens, my wolf finally finished and joined the crowd in silence. A flash rang out, followed by an explosion of twinkling of lights signifying the arrival of Jasmine and her spirit companion. Two small stars, clustered together with others, twinkled fiercely before gradually diminishing. A moment later and the night sky began to take on its usual appearance—stars resurfaced and the moon returned to its place. Noise began to creep back in as the creatures and insects moved about. The ritual was over. Everything was ready to move on.

The witch's fire died down, revealing the absence of Jasmine's body, leaving only the unblemished shroud and flowers behind. One by one, the pack moved about. First passing by Vivien as a token of gratitude for her officiating, and then we each silently went our separate way to shift back into human form.

I followed closely behind Mason before heading back to the room together. We changed without speaking, occasionally stopping to touch one another as we dressed. There was no need for words; we wore our hearts clearly for the other to see. One quick kiss and we headed back out to the garden. It was time to celebrate the girl we both loved and show that even though the pain lingers, the Mystic Wolves would survive.

Chapter Fifteen

The atmosphere was definitely lighter as we emerged from the house. The gravity of the rite was tenderly placed aside for a more casual appearance, tables set out where the chairs had once been. Alongside the walkway, a delicious feast was in the process of being arranged by a small group of Vivien's associates.

Whispering to Mason I'd return, I made my way through the tables, checking to see that everyone was alright and was getting enough to eat. We were a solemn bunch, talking softly amongst ourselves and the ritual was on everybody's mind.

I lingered by some of the conversations, reaching out to touch those I spoke with, letting them know how grateful I was they were here. Soon, the reverent hush became lighter, as laughter broke out and as I caught Mason's eye, I smiled and nodded. We were all okay.

Walking over to where the food was displayed, I helped an older pack sister fill her dish. She shared different experiences she had with Jasmine, how the young wolf touched her life, and as I led her to her table, I thanked her. The topic of dinner shifted, and the air filled with an assortment of memories. It felt like a warm, comfortable blanket settled over the group, and I leaned into Mason, as he came up behind me.

"Have you gotten something to eat yet?" I asked, turning around so I could face him. Telltale signs gave away how tired he was, and I traced the skin under his eyes before standing on my tiptoes to kiss him. "How about you go take a seat by Daniel and let me wait on you a little?" Not giving him time to answer, I gently pushed him in the right direction before turning to grab him a plate of food.

There was so much to select from, so I chose a little of everything I knew he liked. Making sure to pick up utensils and a napkin, I made my way over to where he was. Mason's head was down in quiet conversation, and I smiled as I watched his best friend reach out and pat his arm.

It was hard not to worry about Mason. As much as I was hurting from all this, I knew he was just as devastated, but wasn't able to lower his guard too much. He needed to be strong for the pack, especially in light of what we'd learned at the meeting. Watching him enjoy his company, and the brief respite, I was determined to make sure I was there in any way I could.

Placing the food in front of him, I smiled as he moved his leg and gestured for me to sit on his knee. I enjoyed sitting this close, finding his touch soothing.

"Looks good, sweetheart," He shared, as he leaned forward to see what I'd brought. Taking in an appreciative sniff, he touched my knee and added, "Smells amazing as well."

I reached over to fill his glass with water, careful not to spill any over the nicely arranged decorations. Someone had displayed floral centerpieces, surrounding them with the rich green foliage of our woods. The one in front of me was beautifully created, the result of a talented individual.

Finally situated, I quietly pushed the fork towards Mason's hand and was rewarded with a burst of laughter from Daniel. Startled by the sudden noise, I wasn't sure whether to glare at him or ask what was so funny.

"Well, my Liege, should I step in a cut your meat for you?" He stretched toward the plate, gripping his own knife and before I could move, Mason whipped out his hand and slapped away his friend's.

"Touch it at your own risk," he growled, shifting the plate away from him. Turning to me he added, "Don't mind him, Darcy. He's just jealous he doesn't have anyone to make sure he eats." Placing a brief kiss on my cheek, he whispered into my ear. "I love it when you take care of me. Thank you."

Sticking my tongue out at Daniel, I placed my hand on Mason's chest and answered. "It's my pleasure. I enjoy making sure you're happy." Wearing a stern expression, I pointed my finger at the bratty wolf. "You better make sure you eat up too, Mister. Don't make me come over there and hand feed you!"

This won a round of chuckles and snort in response. "As if you could."

My eyebrow instantly arched and I went to move. He must've thought better of it because he picked up his own fork and began eating, mumbling about how he didn't need another mother. I smiled at him sweetly, before popping a piece of cucumber from Mason's plate into my mouth.

"You can call me your Royal Highness, if you like. That, or Queen Darcy, Ruler Supreme," I suggested, enjoying the moment to tease.

"How about Empress Bossy Boots? That has a nice ring to it." Daniel smirked as he smeared a piece of meat with sauce, taking a bite.

"Only if you have a death wish, Brother,"

Mason replied, filling my mouth with a cherry tomato from his salad before I could answer.

I narrowed my gaze at him as I bite into the fruit with my teeth. Bossy boots indeed, I thought and I shook my head. Daniel knew me so well, and I winked at him.

Feeling the need to move around, I noticed desserts being brought out, and the resulting grumble in my stomach had Mason helping me off his lap.

"Does anyone else want something sweet?" Straight away I saw nods from them both, and heard the request for chocolate.

Kissing Mason on the cheek, and slapping Daniel on the arm for being a punk, I zigzagged my way through everyone and almost sighed at the sight of the table. It was laden with so many delicious things, my sweet tooth felt like rejoicing.

I felt someone touch my elbow, and turning around, I found myself facing one of Vivien's friends. "Thank you so much for everything. We appreciate all the hard work you've put into preparing this." I grasped hold of her small hand and shook it slightly. "It means a lot, and I know Mason will want to thank you personally."

The young woman, possibly in her early twenties, blushed and smiled shyly. "Oh, there's no need to thank us. It's the least we could do to show our respect." Looking around at the contented crowd, she added. "My name's Lily. I actually came over to ask you something. We had a little accident and were wondering where you keep your cleaning things. I hate to interrupt, but I didn't want anyone to trip and fall."

"Oh, no problem. Let me go get you some supplies. Where will you need them?" I stood on my tiptoes and strained to see if I could spot the area.

"Please, no. I'll take care of it. I don't want to pull you away from the meal." Lily's forehead wrinkled into a frown and she looked concerned.

"It's no worry. It'll only take me a few minutes and it's easier than me giving you directions." I touched her arm, reassuringly. "Honestly, it's okay. I don't mind." After repeating back where I needed to meet her, I headed into the house. Hopefully, what I was looking for was where I'd last seen it. It'd been a long day, and I was anxious to spend more alone time with Mason.

Arriving in the laundry, I began looking around for the dust pan and brush. It was the distinct cough of someone that pulled my attention back to the present. I glanced up, startled to find a man a few steps away, a knowing smile on his face.

"Can I help you?" I queried, unsure of who he was. I wasn't going to assume in knowing all of Mason's acquaintances, but there was something about this person I couldn't quite put my finger on.

"Oh, I'm sure you can, Darcy." I didn't like the smug way he looked at me or how he spoke my name as though we were intimately connected. I took a step backward, attempting to put some distance between us. I felt reasonably safe with all the pack members and guests just outside, but I couldn't deny the way my wolf had instantly awakened. She sensed danger, and so did I.

"If you're looking for Mason, he's outside. Here let me take you to him." I moved quickly, aiming toward the door and protection. I miscalculated a step, banging my hip against the washing machine, and I yelped in surprise. Rubbing my side, and ignoring the pain as it throbbed, I kept my eyes focused on the stranger. But even doing that, I didn't see him move until it was too late.

His hand lashed out, grabbing hold of mine, and he pulled me toward him. I raised my arm to push him away and break free of his grasp, but it was like trying to pry off steel fingers. He was strong, painfully strong, and I gasped when I looked up into his face. I tried again, only to find myself captured.

"Let me go!" I put all my weight behind my body as I shoved, and was met with brute resistance. "Who the hell are you?"

My wolf was rushing to the surface, chomping at the bit, and I sent a message for her to wait a moment. She was ready to take over and eliminate this new threat, but I needed to know who this person was, and why they were here.

"Tsk-tsk ... such a mouth, Darcy." He shook his head as if disappointed with me, and it only served to infuriate me more. I struck out with my foot, kicking him hard in the shin. His grip remained iron clad. He didn't even flinch.

"Yes, you will do perfectly. What fun we're about to have." He chuckled to himself before using a commanding tone. "Darcy. Look at me." Compulsion filled the air, magic trying its best to persuade me.

Vampire. I instantly closed my eyes, and I fought the urge to look at him. The weak were easily swayed just by hearing the coercive tone of voice, but for most supernatural creatures, it required direct eye contact. I opened my mouth to scream, and signaled for my wolf to change.

"Oh, no you don't, my lovely."

I felt my body being shaken with such incredible force my eyes flew open, and any thought I had was instantly rattled silent. Gripping hold of my face, our eyes locked, and contact with my wolf came to a halt. I couldn't sense her—couldn't sense anyone. It was just me and the stranger in front of me.

"You will not change. You will not contact your future mate or pack members. You will come with me quietly, and offer me no resistance. What I say, you will do. You won't speak, or move, unless directed. Nod if you understand." He was authoritative, and my head nodded automatically. I was completely at his mercy.

"Perfect." He smiled, and taking hold of my elbow began leading me toward the front door. No one saw us, everyone was still in the backyard, and there was no breaking the spell of persuasion I was under.

He hurried us over to his car, sliding me into the front seat and getting in behind the wheel. He locked the doors, turning the ignition before looking at me again.

"Put your seat belt on, Darcy. You are precious cargo." My hands moved on their own, the sound of the buckle clicking into place loudly. My head hit the back of the seat as my now captor stepped on the gas, and pulled away from the curb. I tried to look at him accusingly, and he smiled at me as if we were the best of friends going for a fun ride.

"By the way, my name is Avery." He reached over and stroked my leg, lingering long enough to make my skin crawl. I willed my hand to move, but was powerless. "This is for your own good. Show me you can behave, and when we get to our destination, I'll lift some of the compulsion."

I glared at him again, causing him to frown.

"I won't have you looking at me that way. Not when we'll be such good friends." Squeezing my leg hard, I knew I made a mistake when I caught his gaze again. "Sleep."

I don't even think I heard the full word before darkness descended and I was gone.

Chapter Sixteen

Whatever I was resting on didn't feel familiar, and the emptiness inside my mind caused me to panic. It took me a few moments to remember what happened, my eyes scanning around the small room trying to gather as much information as possible. I attempted to send a message to Mason, to show him images, but it caused pain in my head, leaving me whimpering.

"I told you no messages, did I not?" A seductive voice floated through the air. Following the sound, I noticed my captor lounging on a chaise as if he didn't have a care in the world. I went to move, but found my body anchored to the bed I was laying on, propped up by pillows. No restraints bound me, the weighty feeling a result of the compulsion.

I opened my mouth to speak and was infuriated when I couldn't. He had complete control and it lit a fire in me. I shot dagger filled looks, ranting at him with my thoughts while he sat there and yawned as if bored.

Swinging his legs so his feet rested on the floor, he stood and moved toward me. "Did you enjoy your rest, Darcy? For someone whose been kidnapped, you sure did sleep a long time. I say a good two or three hours. I'd venture a guess the entire Pack is in uproar, tearing apart Woodside Hollow looking for you." He brushed his hand down the length of his leg, as if dusting himself off. "I know I would if you were mine. You really are exquisite." I hated watching him reach out and touch me, knowing I couldn't do anything to stop him.

"I can see why Mason is so taken with you." His fingers traced a path up my side, slowing briefly by my breast before continuing upward. He placed his palm against my cheek, leaning in to smell the side of my neck. "As I've sat here and watched you sleep, a question has plagued me. I wonder what you taste like?"

I willed myself to remain calm, not wanting him to have the satisfaction of knowing how scared I was. The last thing I wanted was to become food for a vampire, a toy to be played with before killing. Regardless of his intent, I didn't see myself walking out of this alive.

Images from the meeting sprung up in my mind along with the realization this was the person behind everything. He must have sensed it, been able to read the horror in my eyes, because it caused him to pull away, tossing his head back in laughter.

"Finally figured it out? I wondered how long it would take. You don't know how impatient I get sometimes while I wait for everyone else to catch up. Oh, come now, there's no need to look so angry. What is two deaths when there is so much to gain?"

I swear I wouldn't have been surprised if he'd added an evil chuckle on the end of his ramblings. Oblivious to the fact I'd yet to answer him, Avery began pacing back and forth alongside the bed.

"So do you know why you're here?" I watched him come to a stop, glancing at me, waiting for a response. "Any idea?" Annoyance flashed before a look of understanding crossed his face. "You may speak, Darcy."

I inhaled sharply as I found my voice, the sound

shaky to my ears. Pausing to draw in strength, I spat out my request. "Release me."

"But we are getting on so well. Are you not enjoying yourself? I know I am. Now where were we? Yes, I asked you a question and you failed to answer me. I warn you not to disappoint me. I've been known to have a temper. Just ask dear Vanessa."

"I have no idea why you brought me here, other than it's something to do with Mason and you wanting to send a message. All kidnapping me is going to do is piss him off, and no one's fury comes close to his. If you hurt me, he will hunt you to the end of the earth and tear you apart—painfully and slowly."

"Oh, such confidence in your Alpha. Such a pity it is misplaced." Avery crooned, his voice mocking.

"I know my Mason. He will not rest until you're destroyed. By killing Jasmine and Vanessa, then taking me, you've signed your death warrant. And if by some act of insanity, he doesn't get you, Devlin and his enforcers will be gunning for you. That's not just confidence. It's fact." I knew I sounded cocky, but it was everything I could not to make my voice shake and reveal my bluff. Not that I wouldn't be avenged, but that I wasn't afraid. I wanted to keep him talking for as long as it took for everyone to find me.

"You talk a convincing game, Darcy. Such a shame your fear wafts around in the air like a heady aphrodisiac. By all means, continue to fool yourself if it makes you feel better. It is definitely entertaining to watch." He moved his hand about in the air, gesturing for me to go on. Sitting down on the side of the bed, he rested his hand on my leg, the pressure of it wreaking havoc on my skin.

"Why don't you tell me why I'm here then? Instead of just killing me, why bring me to some room and talk?" I tried to put a pleasant tone to my voice, but it was hard speaking through clenched teeth. My attitude was lost on Avery, however, as he beamed back at me, obviously delighted in himself. All I could think was I was alone with a mad man and had no way of escaping.

"You know, I have been a neglectful host. Here we are chatting and not once have I asked after your wellbeing. Would you care for something to eat or drink?" As he licked his lips, the tips of his fangs revealed, he chuckled. "I know I would not say no to a little sip."

Fear shot through me, the idea of him biting me causing bile to surge up my throat into my mouth. There was a lot of ways to be violated, and this was one in my mind. I wasn't opposed to the concept of sharing blood—it was the idea of someone tapping my vein without my consent that caused my stomach to churn.

"No?" he paused, waiting for the answer I wasn't going to offer. "So I guess we will just talk business then, shall we? Get down to the nitty-gritty of why you are here."

"Can you release me at least? Give me the opportunity to move and stretch?" I knew it was a long shot, but I was tired of sitting like a helpless duck. I was used to being a predator, the creature who struck fear in the weaker, and there was nothing comforting about being the prey.

"For you to attack me? Escape? Don't insult my intelligence, Darcy. You will remain how you are until I say otherwise. Besides, our time together is short. Let us not waste it on requests you know I will not approve."

Avery pulled himself to a stand again, turning to face me as he would a crowd. I inwardly rolled my eyes, hoping he wouldn't begin grandstanding and give over to dramatics. Fervor seemed to strike him as he began his story.

"You, my delightful girl, are the perfect pawn in my plan. Do you know how insufferable it is to watch a fool govern over my people, leading us away from the old ways because he feels it is best to keep hidden? Vampires were never meant for the shadows, yet as the centuries pass by, that is exactly where we are. We do not reveal ourselves—we no longer keep humans as the slaves they truly are. We do not bend others to our supreme will, and as a result, we have become weak creatures to be mocked and laughed at."

The look of disgust covering his face was the first real indication Avery wasn't all charm and madness. He had a glint in his eye that drove home how dangerous he was. Whatever show of hospitality he'd been performing earlier was lost now as his true nature was exposed.

"If you're so upset by the way things are, why haven't you done something about it?" I couldn't help the question. Up until the last day, I never heard of Avery before, and if he was all about domination, surely news of his attempts would have filtered through the supernatural community.

"Oh, I've tried, but to no avail. One thing about my kind is we can afford to be patient and not act rashly. We have an eternity to plot and put our plans in motion. The last time I made a serious attempt, I was foiled by the mistimed alliance with Zane, and a young, foolish Alpha."

"Mason ...," I whispered, trying to remember what I'd heard a few years ago when the agreement to join forces had been put into place. It was spoken of as the turning point in our history because instead of everyone working separately, and most times against each other, leaders had met and agreed to pull together.

"Yes, if it were not for him, my ploys at stirring up the factions would have succeeded. I would be the one sitting on the throne, my will being enforced. So you see it's quite simple really. Mason breaks his alliance with Zane, bows down before me, and with him brings the rest into humble submission."

"You're mad if you think he'll agree to those terms."

"I know he will agree to join me because you underestimate your complete value. I have chipped away at his resolve by killing his sister and childhood sweetheart. Should I hurt you, it will break him even more, make him easier to bend and mine for the controlling."

"So why not just kill me? If your whole plan revolves around brainwashing him, why prolong it?" I knew I was tempting fate by talking of my death, but I wanted to know—needed to know exactly what we were up against.

"Because I am almost certain your death will utterly damage him, therefore making him useless to me. No, I want him to see I hold all the power, and only his obedience to my commands will keep you with him."

He looked so arrogant, standing there as if he had it all figured out, but I didn't point out the blatant flaw in his plan. Mason would never bow. Yes, my death would crush him, but there was an amazing strength and resilience to the man I loved. It wouldn't be long before he rose and focused his entire attention on seeking justice. I knew love made people do crazy things, and it could also make them feel like they're buried deep in a pit of despair when lost. But never take from a wolf because eventually they will bite back, heading straight for the throat. Avery was a fool for not recognizing that.

"So now you have me, what do you plan on doing with me?" Everything hinged on this answer.

"Are you eager to part ways, Darcy? I'm hurt." He held his hand to his heart and slightly bowed his head, a mocking look of distress on his face. "What would you say if I told you I hoped to keep you by my side ... indefinitely?"

I tried to school my expression as he studied my face, capturing my eyes.

"Not going to answer my questions? Fine, it seems you no longer need your voice. Do not speak further." The compulsion hit hard and I found myself mute once more.

All I felt was a slight breeze to indicate he'd moved. One moment he was standing away from me and next, he had his mouth at my throat, fangs grazing back and forth over my pulse. I froze as I waited for the telltale pricks on my skin to say he'd bitten me.

"You are so easy to taunt, my sweet. There will be no biting today. In fact, as I told you earlier, our time together is short. I will return you to your beloved Mason, and I trust you'll share with him everything I've told you. You will be my message." He trailed his face alongside my neck, taking in a deep breath before brushing against my ear. "You are so tempting. Maybe I should take a little sample—one for the road as they say."

I felt him nip at my ear lobe, his teeth breaking skin and I tried to block out the sensation of him sucking briefly. He groaned with pleasure, my blood obviously appealing to him and I began to fervently pray that a sample was all he truly wanted.

"Interesting, Darcy." He pulled back, a look of surprise on his face. "Is there something you wish to share?" I felt my brows furrow in confusion as he continued. "Hmmm ... mystery and beauty. I shall enjoy this indeed. Now sleep."

Before I could reason out what his cryptic comments meant, I was pulled back into darkness.

The first thing I noticed was my ability to move, and next the incessant pacing of my wolf. Before I could act and see why things had changed, I heard a loud noise which sounded strangely like a door being ripped off its hinges.

"Where is she?" the voice demanded.

"Mason?" I finally opened my eyes and found myself surrounded by the familiarity of my bedroom. Looking around the concerned faces of Devlin and Daniel, I saw a much disheveled Alpha storming towards me. Scooping me up in his arms, crushing me against his chest, he practically bellowed for an update.

"I'm not sure what happened. No one saw her come back, or any sign of who took her. One minute her room was empty, and next April came running out screaming she was here. I've asked those who've been patrolling the grounds and they all say the same thing—they saw nothing." Daniel spoke firm and clearly, delivering his report.

I went to speak and share where I'd been, but it was as if I was invisible, the men talking over me and amongst each other.

"What about now? Who's looking for any indication of the intruder? Someone can't just waltz in and out of here, however they damn well please, or whenever they feel like it." Mason's roar made me flinch with its intensity. "I want this entire place put on extreme lock down. No one breathes without me knowing. Do you understand?"

"Yes, Mason. I've already issued the alert."

"Heads will roll if this happens again. Whoever this is doesn't know who he's dealing with." Mason turned slightly before continuing. "It goes without saying this person is mine. No interference from you, or your Enforcers. I want full authority to deal with the culprit myself."

I could feel the tension building in Mason—he was like a tight string of elastic ready to snap at any second.

"No one questions your right," Devlin answered. "You may want to let Darcy down, however. I'm pretty sure she has things to share, and your crushing her is only preventing her from breathing. She's safe, Alpha."

"Don't presume to tell me what to do, vampire."

I was shocked at the hostility I heard. I'd never heard Mason speak like that before—especially to someone he counted as a close friend.

"Do not let your anger and frustration cloud your judgment, wolf. I am not your enemy. I am, as always, amongst your friends. I'm merely pointing out the fact she has tried to speak, but is not being heard. Now is not the time to give in to your temper."

It was a testament to their friendship as I felt the man I love step back, the struggle just under his skin as he reined himself in. Not many people would get away with speaking to the Alpha that way without facing consequences.

Suddenly, I was being transferred into a different set of arms—Daniel's. I turned to look toward Mason. He was shaking with power, running his fingers through his hair, his eyes practically blazing with the sign of his wolf. He was fighting instincts, the need to kill and maim, and I reached out to him through our connection.

I'm okay. I'm safe. I tried to infuse my words with all the love I had. I hated seeing him so riled up, his control hanging in the balance, but either my message never reached him or he was too far gone. I gestured for Daniel to lower me to the ground, thanking him and Devlin for being here before returning to sit on the edge of my bed to wait.

Mason finally calmed, his fists unclenching, but he still carried a hardened expression on his face—the Alpha ever present, the man who was my lover and mate off to the side.

Glancing around to the others, I took in a deep breath and began relaying Avery's message. Once I was done, there was a brief lull of silence before all three exploded into action, a mass of comments and curses flying. Having everything out in the open showed just how serious the matter had become.

Devlin excused himself, phone all already out and his king's number being dialed. Daniel was listening intently to Mason as he ordered for everyone to meet again to discuss and come up with an effective strategy. Each had a task to perform—all but me.

"What would you have me do, Mason?" I looked up expectantly. I knew there wasn't much I was able to do, but I wanted to be useful. Not just as his future mate, but as a member of the pack.

I was taken aback when he growled at me. "You can stay in your room, with guards at your door and window until I deem it's safe for you to leave."

I snorted, shaking my head slightly. "I understand your concern. Really I do, but keeping me a prisoner isn't going to solve this, and I honestly don't think Avery is going to return for me. He's delivered his message, I've served my purpose. He'll be waiting for your response now. Let me help." I reached out to touch him, my hand resting gently on his arm. "I'm safe. We didn't know what we were facing and now we do. It'll be okay."

He shook his head. "I thought you were safe before, Darcy. Here in our home and on pack land. No one should've been able to get to you, but he did. I know you don't think so, but I can't think if I don't know every precaution has been taken."

"I agree with being careful. I don't ever want to be taken from you again, but please don't turn me into another hostage. If it gives you peace of mind, assign someone to stay with me when you can't. Just let me move around if I want. Don't put me in a gilded cage." I added an extra layer of pleading to my voice. I needed to reach him.

"Fine, just no leaving the property. I don't mean to be insensitive, I just want you safe. I need to know I can find you whenever I want to be able to touch and see you. Avery may have a death wish coming after me, but he knows enough to recognize you as my Achilles heel. I refuse to lose you."

He pulled me into another embrace, this one much gentler than the last. I could feel his heartbeat pounding inside his chest, adrenaline causing his body to prepare itself. There would be no relaxing or lazing about together until this was over. I stretched upward to place a kiss on his lips, hoping he'd take the bait and give in to a few moments of savoring each other, but he offered back a perfunctory peck before releasing me.

"Stay in your room until I can find someone. It shouldn't take long, and then you're free to roam. I also want you checking in with me every hour on the hour. No texting. I want to hear your voice."

I tried hard not to roll my eyes at what I saw as

225

overkill, and nodded. He left without touching me, his mind elsewhere, and I let a sigh as I looked around my room. What was I possibly going to do while I waited?

Remembering the romance novel I only read half way through, I flopped myself on my bed and got comfortable. Finding the place my book mark was protecting, I willed myself to focus on the story and the happily ever after the hero and heroine were desperate for.

I just hoped I still had one of my own.

Chapter Seventeen

A sharp knock was all the notice I got before Daniel poked his head though the door, asking if it was safe to enter. Despite my doubts, the hour had flown by quickly and I was grateful the book had held my attention so completely. Having already called Mason, I was eager to get out of the room so I quickly placed the book mark and returned the novel to my bedside table.

"Of course, it's safe to enter. What were you expecting? World War Three or something?" I laughed at the look of surprise on his face as he glanced around my room.

"I was at least expecting a few broken things. You know, from throwing them at that stubborn alpha of ours after he laid down the law." Obviously not finding what he was hoping, he looked back at me, shaking his head. "Now, now Darcy, where is your female indignation from being ordered about? Tell me there were at least tears? Threats? Pouting?"

"You're a dork!" I laughed, punching him in the arm. He flinched, rubbing the spot, acting as though I'd given him a mortal wound. "Oh come on, that couldn't have hurt. You're such a ham, Daniel."

Laying off the theatrics, he stopped and suddenly looked serious. "Of course not. I was merely trying to make you feel better." A slow smile curled his lips and he leaned in for effect. "Besides, has anyone ever told you, you punch like a girl?" He took a large step backwards, avoiding the second swing of my arm by a mile. "See what I mean?"

"How else am I supposed to hit, Daniel? Hello ... I am a girl!" I used my hands to show my body. "Is this why you don't have a girlfriend? Are you confused about what we look like?" I squealed out loud as he reached out to swat me, and I tried my best to block him. My arm went wide, resulting in the painful sting of his hand connecting with my side.

"Crap, Darcy. Do you not know how to defend yourself?" His cheeky grin now turned incredulous.

"I'm a werewolf. I always assumed I had the natural ability to take care of myself. I didn't think it was it was that important," I paused.

"Until now." All joking was gone as Daniel finished my sentence.

"Yeah. I didn't like how it felt being so defenseless. Avery cut me off from my wolf completely. I was helpless against his compulsion." I looked up to find eyes filled with compassion. "I don't want to feel like that again."

"Then that's what we'll work on." He offered no more explanation as he took hold of my hand, leading me from my room and out of the house. He kept a brisk, steady pace as we made our way to the back of the property, to the space where Mason had a gym installed.

Throwing the doors wide open, Daniel made quick work of turning on the lights, revealing a place filled with every kind of fitness equipment you could imagine. I glanced over at the treadmill. That was by far my favorite because I was able to read while I walked and avoid just staring off into nothing. I moved to go climb on it, but I was directed elsewhere.

"Welcome to your first ever lesson in self-defense ... Daniel style."

I raised my eyebrows at the last part of his comment because I had no idea what he meant by it. Judging from the cocky way he stood, I'd say I was in for an education of sorts.

"Ready? Assume the position."

I burst out laughing, my hands covering my mouth. "What position?" I struck a pose and watched his eyes almost pop out of his head.

"Oh, no you don't, I'm being serious. I know I don't have much to work with." He smiled as he walked a slow circle around me, flicking his hand at my ponytail. "But I need to at least show you some basics. This is the position I want you in." He stood in a fighting stance, and I rolled my eyes.

"Why didn't you just tell me to get into a fighting stance? Even I know what it's called." I blew a puff of air upward, moving a stray lock of hair out of my eyes.

I shifted my body until I was standing to the side with my right foot in front. I readjusted my legs, making sure they were a shoulder width apart and I raised both my hands up, curling them into fists. I leaned my weight onto my back leg and was instantly chastised.

"No! Never put all you weight on one leg. Distribute it down in the middle." He moved forward, pushing down on my shoulders, causing me to bend them both. I felt my muscles begin to burn from the sudden tension.

"Why does it matter?" I asked, not sure why I even had to stand this way.

"Straighten your legs again ... like you just had it." I didn't have time to respond before he shoved hard at my chest, sending me flying. Walking over to where I painfully landed, he pulled me up onto my feet. "That's why it's important. By keeping your weight equal, you can maintain balance. How effective will you be at defending yourself if you're sprawled on the floor? The key is to stay upright. Try again."

Dusting myself off, I got back into the stance, this time mindful of my body. I watched him strike out again, and even though he moved me backward, I was able to regain my stability and footing quickly.

"You learn fast, young grasshopper." He smirked before returning to teacher mode. "Now, can you guess why it might be helpful to stand like this?" He moved his body to match mine, legs firmly apart. I studied him for a moment before shaking my head. A few answers filtered through my mind, but I didn't know if I was right.

"What does this tell your opponent?" He raised both his fists, an expression of concentrated focus on his face. He appeared every bit the warrior, and I was glad for his help. Looking him over, I suddenly realized the point.

"It tells them you're ready to defend yourself," I replied as it suddenly seemed obvious to me as he stood there. "You can see every move they'll make and be prepared." His wide grin told me I was right.

"Exactly. Come stand in front of me—right there." He gestured to the open space before him. "Now go slowly, and watch how I move. Throw a punch."

Without hesitation, I let my hand fly and he deflected it away with a frontward block of his wrist. It seemed effortless and as he stepped in close, I noticed I was now free to be attacked. A slight jab to my ribs illustrated that fact.

"See how it opened you up? Try again," he stated.

I threw another punch, this time coming from a

different angle. His block also changed, but the results still the same. I was thrown off balance, exposed enough for him to strike again.

"Now instead of punching, come at me like you are going to grab me."

I went to move and came in contact with his leg. Whether it was the front or back, foot or knee, I repeatedly tried to seize him as I met with resistance.

"Now I need you to promise me—swear to me—the move I'm about to show you, you will never use on me ... no matter how much you might be tempted." There was a twinkle in his eye which made me curious so I quickly agreed. "Chances are those who'll try to assault you will be men, and even though they'll far outweigh you, and perhaps even be stronger, you do hold a few advantages."

I instantly started grinning because I knew where he was going with this. The way he cupped himself was also an indication he was aware I understood.

"I already know I can knee a guy in the balls, Daniel. Hit them hard enough and it makes them fall to their knees, whimpering like a baby. Want me to show you?" I smiled sweetly.

His face whitened before he shook his finger at me in warning. Making sure he was out of reach, he continued. "Don't be afraid to use it if you need to. It does require you to get in close, or at least have decent aim, but you need to make sure you hit hard. Put all your weight and force behind the blow. You want to knock them out of commission long enough for you to get away."

"Okay, full weight ... powerful hit." I started raising my knee, pretending I was facing an attacker and I couldn't help imagining Avery every time I made a strike. I held the perverse need to show him this exact move up close and personal. "What else you got?" I wiped away the sweat on my forehead with the back of my wrist, ready for more.

"Another thing you can do is this." Grabbing hold of my hand, he moved it in a forty-five degree angle, palm open and fingers slightly curved. Tapping the meaty heel, Daniel continued. "Use this part here and aim straight for the person's face." Demonstrating his own, he showed the motion I would need to follow and what I would need to target. "Hit them in the nose with the intent of breaking it. You'll cause their eyes to water, blood to flow, as well as a crap load of pain. Everything I'm showing you is designed to give you time to escape. I don't want you engaging them in combat."

Moving my hand back and forth, helping me get used to the flow of movement, he released me, and I was able to maintain the motion without fault. If the pain I felt when I accidently bumped my nose was any indication, this would definitely hurt. My confidence increased, and I smiled widely.

"One more thing, and then I'm going to have you work on those girly punches." Daniel laughed and with lightning fast reflexes he turned me, pulling me hard against his body, and placing his arms around my neck. "Sometimes your attacker won't give you the courtesy of seeing them coming. Rude, I know, but what can I say? Any person who'll attack a woman doesn't exactly have a strong moral compass. Now, try to get out of this."

He held me in a tight grip and squeezed hard. No matter how much I struggled, all I did was tire myself out, and I became frustrated. I tried bending over to break the hold. I couldn't reach his private parts, and there was no prying him off. I even started to dig my nails into his flesh, but it only made him tense up.

"Remember, if the person is human, you're not

going to have any of these problems. As a werewolf, you automatically hold advantage because of your strength. It's if your attacker is supernatural that you'll need to keep your focus because you'll both share similar abilities. What you need is the element of surprise." He paused a moment before chuckling in my ear. "Given up yet?"

I growled, hanging my hands on his arm to try and alleviate the pressure. "Yes. Show me."

"Okay, there are two things you can do. But first, remember you love me and would hate to hurt me. One, slam your head backward, it's hard and can do a lot of damage. You want to stun them so they'll break their hold."

I repeated his instructions like a mantra. "Head back. Stun. Release. What else was there?"

"Next, lift your leg and smash it down with all you have on their foot." He released me quickly and bent down before me, lifting mine. "Aim here, where there's a curve and your foot attaches to your ankle. You can hit lower and break toes, but you want maximum exposure for pain. Strike hard enough so they'll release you and then run. If you can't just yet, you can turn around and kick them. They may be bent over, trying to protect their foot. You just step in there and knee them in the face. Down they go."

It was a lot to remember, but I got the gist of the basics. I hoped I never need to use any of this, but I realized I'd been foolish in not taking this seriously. I knew Daniel was giving me a crash course right now, but it gave me an idea.

"Do you think we can set something up where you teach me more—maybe weekly lessons? I would really like to learn how to defend myself against weapons." I watched his eyes narrow and him start to shake his head. "Wait, hear me out. I pray I never have to face that kind of situation, but surprise, I did. Gary held me at gunpoint and I can't stop thinking it might've helped if I'd known a few moves. Yes, I could've changed, but I know I still bleed as a wolf. She could've been hurt too."

"Let me talk with Mason first, but I don't see why not. It's a good idea and it never hurts to be prepared. Maybe we can even ask some of the others if they want to join in." He looked thoughtful and I took the moment to stretch out my muscles. I was pretty fit, but the last hour had worn me out a little. Swinging my arms in circles, getting them limber, I pointed toward the punching bag. "Shall we?"

I loved watching people swinging at the leather bag, always wondering when it would break loose from its fixture in the ceiling and go flying. No matter how hard I'd seen Mason and the others hit it though, it was still pretty sturdy.

Maybe I'll be the one to knock it loose. I snorted at the thought.

Daniel threw over a roll of tape with the comments to wrap my hands for protection. I watched as he prepared his own, and I soon had a matching set, moving my fingers to get a feel for it.

"Okay, show me your fists, Darcy." I lifted my hands, curling them inward; making sure my thumb was tucked in properly. He rewarded me with a nod, using his own palm to crunch my fingers in tighter.

"You don't want this loose and sloppy when you throw it. It lessens the force and hurts you more." Pointing me in the right direction, he demonstrated a few punches, showing me the correct way to move before indicating it was my turn.

The impact sent a jarring wave straight up my arm into my shoulder, and I released a small oomph.

Adjusting my stance and realigning my torso, I threw my fist again, and this time, it moved the equipment slightly. I looked over to Daniel triumphantly, and he rolled his eyes.

"Come on, Tyson, keep going." He came and stood behind the bag, holding it firmly between his arms, and offered coaching tips. I put everything out of my mind and soon lost myself to the rhythm of each blow—one after the other. I felt myself begin to work up a sweat.

"Change it up a little. See if you can include some jabs." He instructed me on how to do them, and I tested it out, each strike meeting the target.

I was so focused I almost missed Daniel's next question.

"You know he didn't mean to be so gruff, right?"

"I know," I said, a little short of breath. "That's why I didn't argue. If knowing I'm safe helps put his mind at ease so he can concentrate, then I say guard away. I just wish there was more I could do. He's still grieving, and without even a chance to take a break, he now has to deal with some crazy vampire usurper." I paused from my activity and looked straight at Daniel. "As the Alpha, a lot of people look up to him, expecting him to be the level head in the storm, but I see more. He's also a man who is fully aware of the danger we face, and is afraid of not being able to protect those he loves. Two warring parts of him, so even though it stings a little, I understand." I threw one more punch. "Besides, I can always punish him for it later."

I couldn't help but laugh at the look of curiosity on Daniel's face.

"Don't even ask. A wolf never kisses and tells." Moving to take off the tape, signaling I was done, I headed over to the bench and took a seat. "I just want to be strong for him. Support him in any way I can."

I felt the bench shift a little with the weight of his body resting on it. I bumped my shoulder against my pack brother, a gentle thank you for being there, and we eased into comfortable silence. It felt good to relax for a moment.

"I've known Mason my entire life. Seen him at his best and his worst, but the look on his face when he realized you were gone, I hope I never see that again. To everyone else, they saw their leader step forward and take charge. Behind the scenes though, when it was just the two of us, he looked like a man completely devastated. He's a powerful wolf, one of the strongest and most lethal I know—it's why I'll follow him to the grave. But he also leads with his heart, and your kidnapping was the final straw in a brutal attack. I'm glad you're not giving him a hard time because I know once this is all over, he'll be back to himself." Reaching over to take the ball of used tape out of my hand, he combined it with his own and aimed towards a nearby wastebasket. "He's the best man I know."

"Thank you for being his friend ... for being loyal." I hugged him quickly. "And for sharing with me."

"Sharing what?" A new voice interrupted as Mason entered the gym. He strode into the room, his lengthy step eating up the distance between us. He looked back and forth, waiting for an answer.

"About how much you miss me kicking your ass in here. It's been a while, Brother. Care for a rematch from the last time?" Daniel cocked his eyebrow, a smirk covering his face as he issued a challenge.

"Whatever, we don't have time for that. I came looking for you to let you know we've received another message. Seems we're not fast enough for Avery and he's grown impatient. He's sent an address for me to meet him so we can discuss the shifting of my alliance."

A feeling of doom and foreboding swept over my body, causing a chill to raise goose bumps on my flesh. "Please tell me you're not actually going to go, Mason. It's got trap written all over it. Hell, it's got neon signs blazing." I turned to Daniel, hoping he would help talk some reason into him.

"Not now, Darcy," Mason answer was short, his attention focused. "And don't think I didn't notice the lack of phone call from you." Addressing his second in command, he added, "I'll need you to get ready. The meeting's set for two hours, but I want to do a little recognizance first—see what we're up against before attacking. I want you loaded up with weapons, but I'm ordering you not to kill unless it's absolutely necessary. He's mine, and I want the pleasure of destroying him."

Having been surrounded by werewolves my entire life, violence was something I was familiar with, but as I listened to the blood thirsty tone in Mason's voice, it was hard to get used to. Here was the man who could sweet talk me like no one else, who could reduce me to a puddle of desire, so the cold steel that edged his words seemed completely foreign.

"Can't you wait? Take more to plan. Call more people. I don't like the feel of this." My anxiety levels increased, and my wolf was also agitated. I'd spent hours with the vampire and I couldn't help worry about his intentions.

"No, we're at war. We need to act, and as Alpha it's my duty to take every opportunity to ensure the safety of my pack. You should know this more than anyone."

"But at the expense of your own safety though

... and that of Daniel? I know what you want and why, but how much clearer do I need to be ... I feel like something bad is going to happen at this meeting. You can't trust Avery."

"I'm not a fool to go in blind."

His anger rose, and I desperately wanted to pull back. I didn't want to challenge his authority, or his ability to lead. I loved this man so much and it broke my heart to keep pushing, but I felt so strongly about this, I thought I would choke. I just knew if I didn't speak up, get him to acknowledge what I was saying was worth listening to—there was a very real possibility of losing him. I needed him. The pack needed him. The Mystic Wolves would be devastated without Mason.

"Take her back to her room to meet her new guard, and I'll see you in fifteen minutes to go over our plans." He put heavy emphasis on his last word, staring at me with such a force, I felt glued to the spot.

Tears sprang into my eyes, as frustration filled me. He wasn't going to listen. "Mason ...."

"Enough," he roared, the loudness of his voice piercing the air. One look at him told me there was no reaching him. He had completely shut himself off, allowing full rein to his instincts, and I lowered my head in submission.

Thanking Daniel for his help, I began backing away toward the door so I could return to my room. I heard sharp whispers, a thud as someone was hit, followed by the words, "Don't be a jerk."

"Wait." Mason's shout brought me to a stand-still. I remained where I was as he ran up behind me before I turned to face him. Gazing up, I still saw the hardness, but I could also see regret. Leaning in, he brushed his lips against mine and promised he'd stop in to see me before he left.

I nodded, not able to speak quite yet, and I could

see Daniel shaking his head in the background. Caressing the side of Mason's face, feeling him lean slightly into my touch, I offered him a smile. "See you then."

Not waiting for his answer, I turned again and left.

Chapter Eighteen

The stillness of my room felt somewhat stifling, the last few moments with Mason playing over and over in my mind. Not caring that someone would be here shortly, I began stripping off my sweaty clothes, the need for a shower the only thing I could concentrate on.

I knew he was under pressure and that even the strongest had their limits. I had confidence he'd be able to face whatever challenges he met later. I just couldn't shake the ominous feeling which had nestled itself in the bottom of my stomach. This is where I needed to have faith— to not just say it, but show it.

Stepping under the water, scrubbing away the grime from my recent workout, I tried to focus on the future. There was so much to look forward to—a lifetime of new experiences, and my highly anticipated mating. Nothing had changed and something told me when we came out on the other side of this, we'd be stronger for it.

The soft perfume from my body wash mingled with the soothing steam of the hot water, seeping its way into my pores, and I began to calm down. I tried to remember what a wise friend told me a few years ago—a problem always looked bigger when it was the only thing I focused on, and as I rinsed off, I kept reminding myself of the bigger picture. This, unfortunately, wasn't going to be the only time we faced danger together as a couple and pack. It wouldn't be the only time we suffered heartache and uncertainty.

Stepping out of the shower, a new sense of determination filled me. Mason had stood by me, taking precious time to help reinstall my confidence in who I was and my place within the pack. I knew how lucky I was to have him, and I made a mental note—once this was over, I wanted to plan a special evening just for the two of us. We needed some alone time so I could pamper him. Grinning, I felt a pulse of excitement. That's exactly what I'd do.

Quickly dressing, I felt lighter for the first time today. I walked out into my bedroom to find a very large, very amused looking, vampire enforcer sprawled across my bed. His rich chuckle charged the air as he began to read out aloud from my romance novel.

"Oh, Bradley, you're so strong. However will I live without you? Kiss me ... kiss me now and I'll be forever yours. I'm all a tremble waiting for you, my darling." His high pitched attempt at sounding like a female made me forget for a moment to yell at him for teasing and I busted up laughing, my hand covering my mouth.

"Felicity. I'm so glad you've noticed my manliness. Please, touch me. Touch my ...." I watched him flip the book closed, taking a quick look at the cover, and he reopened to the spot his finger marked, "hard muscles and long flowing hair." He snorted, clearly finding it funny and returned the book to its rightful spot.

"Please tell me you don't enjoy that?" He looked at me incredulously, patting the space beside him on the bed as an invitation for me to come sit. "That was cheesy, and it'll turn your brain to rot."

"Hey, don't mock my romance book, and you know that's not what it says either. Go ahead and laugh, but you don't know what you're missing!" I flopped myself down, slapping him for good measure on his leg. "I'm sure it's more fascinating than what you read, Mr. I'm-A-Broody-Vampire. Probably something heavy and extremely tragic." I rolled my eyes at him, mocking him right back.

"You think you're so funny. For your information, I just finished a murder mystery. It was quite entertaining."

"Really?" I turned my head to look at him. He didn't come across as someone who'd be interested in the genre, or any for that matter.

"No. I don't have time for such luxuries, but if I did, it wouldn't be something with the title "Surrendering to the Mistress of Promises." He eyed the book again.

"I'll let you borrow it when I'm done. It'll be our little secret." I tapped him on the leg and got off the bed. Mason still hadn't come by yet, and I was anxious to see him before he left.

"He'll be okay, you know?" I turned around quickly, ready to blast him. "And no, I didn't read your thoughts. I understand you well enough to read your body language. You're worried about the meeting, but Mason's got a smart head on his shoulders. He'll be careful."

"I hope so." I began to slowly pace back and forth, inching closer to the door with each step. As if willing him there, I heard a knock and Mason entered, followed closely by Daniel. They were both dressed in black, weapons concealed, but my focus was solely on the man moving toward me.

He looked lethal and dangerous. I could tell by the game face he was wearing, he was in complete control. Any uncertainty was gone as the full weight of the Alpha mantle rested squarely on his shoulders. He'd take no risks tonight.

"We're ready to head out, sweetheart." The use of the endearment settled some of my anxiety. He seemed balanced, and I stepped into his open arms, ignoring the way the knives he had hidden dug into my skin. I inhaled deeply, enjoying his masculine scent, and I tried to show my support through our embrace.

I was the one who stepped away first, squeezing his hand before looking back at him. "Be safe, okay? Do what you need to do and then come home." I smiled widely, and my heart skipped a beat when he returned one of his own. I saw the look of relief in his eyes.

"I'll try to send you updates through our connection, so you don't spend the rest of the night worrying. I know you have a bad feeling." He reached out and stroked the curve of my face. "I did hear you, even though I acted like I didn't. Daniel and I have gone over every possible scenario we could think of, and if it looks like a trap we'll get out of there. I just can't let this chance slip by. Who knows what lengths Avery will go to if these have been his opening moves?"

"You don't need to explain. I understand, and I appreciate you offering to send updates. Besides, I'll be fine here with Devlin." I gestured over my shoulder to where he was laying. "I know just how we'll spend our evening as well." I could hear Devlin groan softly.

"I love you, Darcy."

My eyes moved over Mason's face, taking everything in. "I love you too," I whispered and I took another step back as he turned to go.

"Keep her safe, Devlin. I'm counting on you. Leave here only if you have to."

"Does this mean you rescind your Alpha command for me to stay on pack property?" I asked.

"Yes, should the need arise, you stay with Devlin. No running off on your own. Promise me, Darcy, or the command stands."

I agreed to his terms, and I felt the burden of the command lift. "I won't leave here by myself. You have my word."

He paused for a moment, weighing things and seemed satisfied. Nodding at Devlin, both Daniel and he left the room.

I let out a heavy sigh, staring at the closed door and I shut my eyes briefly to offer up a heartfelt prayer. Twirling around, I attempted a smile as I settled myself back on the bed. Devlin wrapped his arm around my shoulder, pulling me close, and I rested against him.

"Ah, the joys of waiting." I laughed, breaking the silence. "So, what shall we do?" I tilted my head to the side, peering over at my friend.

"Anything you'd like. I'm at your service, Madam Darcy." He added a flourish with his hand. "Your wish is my command."

"Honestly? I think I'd just like to talk. We don't often get the chance and I've missed you." Devlin had always been a part of my life, showing up from time to time when I needed him or whenever he was in town. As an Enforcer, he travelled the world at the order of his King, but I loved whatever chance I got to be with him when he was home in Woodside Hollow.

"Then fire away. What's the first topic for discussion?"

I loved the way he bantered with me, and I tapped my finger against my chin, trying to decide. There was still so much I didn't know about him because he was the master of evasion. Though I learned not to pry too much into his life, I looked forward to whatever tidbit he revealed. There were things on my mind we could talk about, but an image flashed in my mind. I suddenly sat up straight, turning myself to face him before crossing my legs.

"What is the deal with Vlad? He doesn't seem to be the kind of partner you would have so I know there's a story there. Spill it." I looked at him intently, waiting to see what he'd divulge.

"He is the bane of my existence at the moment ... the thorn in my side ... the constant source of irritation." He rubbed his hand across his forehead, lowering his voice. "And he's also my family."

I couldn't help it. I exploded into laughter so hard I had tears welling in my eyes. "He's your relative?" I was lucky to get the question out.

"Are you finished?" He cocked his eyebrow, a scowl on his face. It seemed I found a tender spot that begged for me to poke at it.

"Nope. I'm sorry, but this is too funny. He appears to be so awkward, and you're always so ... not awkward. How come I've never met him before?"

"Because I never intended him to become a vampire, or to be introduced into our world." He let out a frustrated sigh, and I slanted forward, knowing he was about to reveal something. "He's a descendant of my beloved sister, and was meant to remain human. They all were, but sometimes things happen. Vlad was to remain ignorant of who I was, but after a lapse in my judgment, discovered I was a vampire. He became enamored with the idea of being turned, pestering me relentlessly until I finally decided to just wipe his mind and remove myself from his life. The evening I chose to execute my plans, I arrived at his home to find him dying, lying in a pool of blood. Seems he didn't need me after all, and had found someone to help him. I had no other option but to help finish his transition and ease his passage into his new life. I was honor bound to protect my family, having given a blood-oath to my sister, so I took him back to my King for guidance. He's with me now because his sparkling personality has almost gotten him staked on numerous occasions." Devlin chuckled to himself. "Imagine that?"

"You made a blood oath with your sister?" I couldn't help the surprise in my voice and I'm sure my eyes were as large as saucers. I didn't know too much, but what I did know was a blood oath was one of the most sacred of pledges a person could offer. It was unbreakable, immovable, and very rarely made. It was the tightest of commitments between two people and to break it meant suffering a death too horrible to imagine.

"My, you are observant tonight." He nodded, smiling, a wistful look crossed his face and I knew he was remembering her.

"You remind me a lot of her—the same willful spirit, gentle soul, and playful heart. There are even times where I think you share similar mannerisms. It made loving you, and wanting to watch over you a joy. Hers was a hard life, one I would never have chosen for her, but as a devoted brother, I honored her wishes. She made the mistake of loving the wrong person, became pregnant, and later lost her life in childbirth. The babe lived, but losing her was a devastating blow. From her death bed she requested something of me, demanding I give her a blood oath, and I couldn't refuse her. I left that night to see it begin and have spent the years bound by it. I know I'll spend the remainder of my life fulfilling my promise, even when it means I'm stuck with a family member who thinks he's reached bad ass status by calling himself Vlad." He scoffed as he ran his fingers through his hair before crossing his arms over his chest. "Of course, maybe it's an improvement from his birth name, which was Cuthbert. I called him Bertie for short, which annoyed him to no end."

I snorted. "Really?" I asked, loving the way he was sharing about his family. I couldn't remember the last time he had talked this long about himself. I was almost too hesitant to interrupt. "Well, it could've been worse, you know?"

"How so?" He asked, looking curious.

"He could've called himself Edward, or Jasper. Sparkling is the "in" thing right now."

Devlin groaned loudly. "I would've staked him myself."

Laughing hard, I grabbed my sides as I imagined him chasing poor Vlad around the room with a stake. Just when I thought I could stop, an image of Devlin glittering in the sun filled my mind, sending me into another round of hysterics.

"Now what?" he said, scowling at my laughter

"I was picturing what you'd look like as a Cullen. I think you'd totally rock the sparkle."

"Yeah, enough." He held up his hand, shaking his head. "Next topic."

"Okay, I'm sorry. It was too hard to resist." Taking in a calming breath, I continued, "I love hearing about your past, though. What was your sister's name?"

"Elynor." He sighed. "Even after all this time I miss her. She would have loved you immensely had she known you."

I rested my hand on his arm and squeezed, trying to offer comfort. We settled into another bout of silence, lost in our thoughts, and I was grateful for the glimpse he had given me. I had no problem imagining him interacting with his sister, doting on her, because he'd shown similar affection for me.

I went to ask him more questions, but became

distracted by the images filtering through my connection. Relaxing, trying to steady my emotions so I didn't lose contact, I closed my eyes and concentrated.

Sensing something was happening, Devlin didn't utter a word, the room going still.

It wasn't difficult to understand what Mason and Daniel was experiencing. They had finally arrived at the meeting place, and judging from what details I could see, Avery had invited them to one of the larger homes on the other side of town. This surprised me because I didn't think he was local. Trying to remember the street names, looking for familiar landmarks, I felt a rush of excitement. I knew where they were.

The house appeared to be dimly light, and as they cautiously entered the property, no one was there to greet them or confront them. Again, this was interesting since I was almost certain Avery would've had an entourage of minions.

Daniel apparently thought the same thing because I heard him ask Mason what he thought about the absence of resistance.

Scoping the area and not seeing any movement, the Alpha whispered to stay alert. They continued moving up the pathway toward the entrance, their hands resting lightly on their weapons

"Is everything alright?" Devlin's voice broke my concentration and I quickly nodded, returning my focus to the mental images so I wouldn't miss anything.

"They've arrived and they're not sure what to make of it. They're approaching the front door, but they don't like the lack of guards. It's too quiet."

"Do you recognize where they are?"

I nodded, but didn't answer. Mason was

pounding on the door and both continued to look around warily. I could sense his confusion and the moment when he decided they needed to leave, but the door suddenly opened, revealing Avery.

He was immaculately dressed in a dark blue suit, tailor made from its appearance. He bowed slightly, welcoming them into his home.

I wanted to scream for Mason to follow his gut and come home, not liking the look of satisfaction on the vampire's face, but I forced myself to be silent.

Showing no hesitation, they crossed the threshold, the door slamming shut behind them, and I felt like this was a scene straight from of a horror movie.

Gesturing for Mason and Daniel to follow him, Avery led them into what looked like a parlor, offering them refreshments as though he was a civilized host. Both refused and I wondered if they caught the flash of disappointment on his face. It was lightning fast, buried within seconds, but there nevertheless.

I watched the bantering back and forth, trivial comments and my head began to pound a little. I felt Devlin rest his hand on my knee, the offer of strength, and I took another breath.

Mason's anger was rising, and Avery was laughing. It seemed the vampire had tried to use compulsion, and I watched as Daniel shook his head as if trying to dislodge something. Mason grabbed hold of Daniel, moving to leave, and I could sense his wolf ready to take charge.

"Avery tried to use compulsion and Mason is furious. I think the meeting's over," I whispered. "And the tension I feel, I'm not sure whether it's mine or his. Something's not right, but I don't know what it means." I could feel myself starting to panic.

Instead of fluid motion, the images I was receiving now were more like snap shots. Mason wasn't showing it all, but what I was able to see and feel, terrified me. Everything seemed to come at me quickly—anger, an attack on Avery, a struggle, Daniel disappearing, Mason having the upper hand and moving in for the kill, a blast of confusion, and then suddenly—nothing. My mind went black, our connection broken.

I screamed, frantic to get it back, and I couldn't help but blame myself for it not working. I wrestled with my mind, trying to reconnect again. All I found was emptiness.

I propelled myself off the bed toward my dresser, grabbing my cell phone. I had no idea what happened, but one thing I did know—Mason was in trouble. I quickly dialed his number, hoping he would pick up. The more it rang, the more impatient I got. I needed to reach him, and heaven help the person who tried to stop me.

Hands took firm grip of me, and I ended the call as I whirled around to confront Devlin.

"Let me go. Now." I was not in the mood to be trifled with and I tried to break free of his grasp. He was immovable, and without thinking, I raised my knee to force him to let go.

He easily deflected it. I fought against him and he answered by shaking me so hard I thought my eyeballs would rattle out of my head.

"Quit fighting me, Darcy. I'm assuming something's happened and that's where you're racing off to go, but please, stop for a moment. Explain what you saw so we can take of this together." He kept his voice level, trying to exude as much calm as possible.

"You said "we". Are you telling me you won't stop me?" I looked at him suspiciously, poised to resume fighting for my release. I felt his hands relax and finally let go.

"As if you would listen. Remember, I know you well, there's nothing I could say that would stop you. We need to have a plan, though." He walked over to my closet, pulling out a pair of shoes. He handed them to me and I put them on. Leaving the room, we headed toward the front door.

"I was hoping we could come up with one on our way there. I'm not sure what's happening, but I saw them fight and then the connection was broken. It can mean one of two things—either I broke it, or Mason is in trouble. I hope it's me and I get a call saying they're on their way home, but I can't risk it. All I know, is I need to act. My Alpha and future mate is in danger."

"Even if it means he gets angry at you, and furious with me? I know you're able to leave the house, but I also know he'd never agree to me allowing you to rush to his rescue." He stepped out into the open air and waited for me to join him.

"We'll cross that bridge when we get to it. Now let's go."

Looking around for his car, I was distracted by one of the most beautiful motorcycles I'd ever seen. It was all shiny chrome with black upholstery, and I found myself drawn to it.

"Please tell me this is yours." This was a masterpiece of machinery, and exactly what we needed to get there quickly.

Handing me the helmet, Devlin swung his leg over. He kicked the stand back, balancing the heavy weight between his legs.

Fastening the head gear, I climbed up behind him, wrapping my arms around his body and resting my hands on his stomach. I could feel the difference in our body temperatures—mine resembled a slight fever and his, a cold chill. Ignoring how it caused my hand to tingle, I leaned forward to speak in his ear.

"Why am I the only one wearing a helmet?" I reached up to adjust the strap so it didn't dig into my chin.

"Because I'm a vampire, and invincible," he retorted.

"Well, I'm a werewolf, and being supernatural isn't going to protect your head from being smashed open like an egg on the asphalt." I knocked my knuckles against his head. "Although, you are pretty hard headed and may bounce a little at first."

"There's only one helmet. I wasn't planning on taking you anywhere when I came here, and despite my many abilities, foresight isn't one of them. I'm more concerned with keeping you in one piece than myself. Let me worry, just hold on tight and tell me where we're heading?"

I gave him the address, and without warning, he flipped open his phone.

"We need back up at 325 Hillsdale Road. The Alpha's in trouble." He didn't even wait for a reply before snapping the device shut, and jump starting the bike.

The wheels spun furiously on the gravel, churning it up and we burst forward, causing me to jolt before I had a chance to correct myself. I slapped him for not letting me know his intentions, and I felt the rumble of laughter through his chest.

As the motorcycle roared down the street, bringing us nearer to our destination, all I could do was close my eyes and pray.

I'm coming, Mason. Just hold on.

Chapter Nineteen

"Let's go," I said, as we parked just beyond the property near the end of a long driveway.

Stripping the helmet off, I placed it on the seat, and moved toward a row of hedges. Hiding myself, as I stared up at the house. I still wasn't able to forge another connection with Mason, but I tried to sense him again. Daniel and he were both in there. I just knew it.

"Slow down, Darcy," Devlin said, dragging me to his side. "I told you I'd get you here, but you play by my rules. First thing we're going to do is wait for back up. With more of us, we'll be better prepared for whatever game Avery is playing."

It had been a while since I'd visited this part of town. A place rich in history, it was rumored to be filled with hauntings and strange occurrences, but all I saw was large, expensive houses and beautiful landscaping. As I gazed around at the different kinds of trees, I felt a slight tug around my heart.

Mason.

Taking in a deep breath, centering myself, I relaxed a little to encourage my senses to continue reaching out. Sure enough, after a few moments, I felt a stronger pull, and I knew with a surety, Mason was inside.

I glanced back at Devlin, and saw him reaching into his pocket. Removing his buzzing phone, he answered it, his back now to me. I couldn't wait for him. The longer I did, the more I risked losing the signal.

"We need to go, Devlin. The connection has reestablished. I can feel him." I grabbed the back of his shirt, yanking as I started to move up the driveway.

"We're out of time. Get here as soon as you can." He ended the call, and grabbed my hand, taking the lead. We moved across the lawn, not stopping until our feet hit the front porch. The tug was more insistent now, and with one last careful glance around—finding no one—we entered the house.

As my eyes adjusted to the dim lighting, I was stunned by the opulence of the foyer. Beautifully crafted paintings hung on the wall, one a family portrait, and the other of children playing. A grand staircase stole most of the room's focus, with elegant carvings of rich mahogany, leading up to a second floor.

Looking around, I pondered what direction we should go.

"Which way now, Darcy?" he asked, his stance alert as he gazed about us.

My nose caught a scent. It was faint, but it was definitely werewolf. Leading him to the nearest room, we peered into what looked like a parlor. I instantly recognized it as the room everyone had met in.

"They were here," I spoke, taking a few seconds to check for evidence.

Devlin entered, giving it a quick scan, but I sensed nothing.

Trying not to be discouraged, I went back into the foyer and closed my eyes, Devlin returning to my side.

I dug down deep, channeling all my energy, and without over thinking it, I began to walk, letting my senses direct me. We passed another room, turning down a hallway that led by a kitchen.

We came across a smaller set of stairs—ones that

looked like it would take us to a cellar or basement. The feeling of Mason grew stronger so placing one foot in front of the other, we began our descent.

I tried to tell myself I had nothing to worry about, and I felt the reassurance come from my wolf. She was alert, watching closely to see what would happen. Using the handrail to keep my balance, I finally reached the bottom and found there was a doorway.

There was a loud crash from the floor above, and the sound of voices shouting. Devlin reached for his boot, pulling out a dagger, and moving back toward the stairs, he ordered me to find somewhere to hide.

"Don't come out until I return for you," he called over his shoulder, and taking two steps at a time, I quickly lost sight of him.

Not knowing where to go, I turned around to the door behind me. Pushing it carefully, I cringed as I heard the creaking of rusted hinges, and I waited to see if anything would jump out.

The room was dark, but the tug around my heart grew stronger. I fumbled for the light switch. The bulb flickered on, fading somewhat before surging to full capacity, and I found myself standing in storeroom where the owners kept food and other household items.

It was a large room filled with row after row shelves, and I walked in further, looking for a place to hide. Coming around one of the shelves, I gasped.

Mason was manacled to the wall, a blank expression on his face.

I gave into my first instinct, racing over to him, feeling for injuries while trying to figure out how to break him free of the cuffs around his wrists. They held his arms out straight, and I could only imagine the pressure it was placing on his shoulders. I whispered words of love, asking him to hold on. Reaching for the restraints, I recoiled back instantly the second my skin came in contact with the metal.

Silver. Avery was holding Mason hostage with the one substance known to burn a werewolf, as well as draining their strength, and preventing from shifting. As I looked closer, tears filled my eyes to see the angry red skin and blisters weeping on his wrists. I knew they had to hurt, but he didn't utter a single sound.

I took hold of his face, moving it back and forth, and noticed his eyes didn't follow me. I spoke loudly, calling his name, but his expression remained empty.

"He is compelled, sweet Darcy, and completely under my control. I could not have him run off and spoil the party, now could I? Where would the fun be if you were not here to watch?"

Avery stepped out from around one of the shelves, smiling widely at my surprise. He looked pleased with himself, and I released a low growl of warning.

"Oh, come now, there is no need for that. Your beloved Alpha is still alive, maybe a little worse for wear, but still breathing." He chuckled as he glanced over at the body hanging on the opposite wall. "I rather like my new decoration."

"Let him go. There's no need to keep him like this. There was no need for any of this."

"Oh, there definitely was, my beauty. You see, after I took you home, I had a change of heart, an epiphany if you will. I discovered I do not really need your Mason as much as I thought I did." He began pacing slowly before me, a look of determination on his face, and I placed myself in front of Mason as a shield.

My wolf began to howl, sensing danger, and we both watched as Avery paused. He seemed to be waiting for something—listening—and with a small sigh he began to shake his head. "Once again, our time is cut short. Oh well, I will do what I must."

A sense of relief brushed over me as I hoped Devlin was returning. I expected him to burst through the door at any moment, and was disappointed when he didn't appear.

"No one is coming, my dear—at least not who you are wanting. If I am right, whoever came with you is now engaged with my guards and I have trained them well." He looked at his fingernails, feigning boredom.

"So where were we? Ah ... yes." He moved quickly, a gust of air revealing his speed, and I found myself staring deep into his eyes. I closed mine, fighting the urge, knowing if I looked I would be under his influence again.

"Look at me, or I will kill your lover." His tone was serious and cold, removing all doubt to his sincerity.

Glaring back, I slowly raised my eyelids. "I hate you," I uttered.

"You have not begun to hate me, Darcy, but do not worry. In a few seconds, you will forget and all you will know is that my touch brings you pleasure."

"You're fooling yourself." I called on my wolf instantly, trying to bring her to the surface. Before I could shift, Avery grabbed onto me roughly. I wasn't able to finish the change as he spoke a few words, the compulsion cutting me off completely.

I felt all resistance to him melt away, and it was replaced with the sudden urge to wrap myself up in him. I couldn't keep my hands from reaching out and stroking him, each time I did, it felt like electricity traveling through my body, covering me with tingles.

I wanted him—needed him—and as I began to rub myself against his body, he whipped me around so my back was against his chest.

"Calm yourself, I'm not ready for you to become so playful. We do not have our audience yet." Leaning forward, he uttered more words, and a surge of energy burst through Mason. His roar of fury bounced off the walls until it was almost deafening.

He strained against the manacles binding him, but they held firm, the clasps refusing to open.

I was worried and began to argue for his release, but a finger brushed down the side of my neck, causing goose bumps to cover my skin. I was lost in a moment of bliss.

My voice was screaming inside my head to ignore his touch, quickly realizing it was the contact which made me lose my reason. I was grateful he hadn't removed my ability to think and I tried to focus, hoping to find a way around the compulsion.

"Let us go, Avery. Whatever you're planning, you can't expect it to work. Regardless of what you do to us, Zane will never abdicate to you. He'll crush you without a moment's thought. The people love him and will follow him. You can't possibly win."

"But I told you I had a new plan, one that involves you." He brushed his lips against my neck, and before I could gag, I convulsed with desire. My body rebelled against me, and no matter what I willed it to do, it wouldn't listening.

"I'm the one you want," Mason shouted, his eyes never leaving me as he watched me in the embrace of another. "You have no need for Darcy. Release her, and I'll do what you ask." He sounded every inch the Alpha as he hung there defenseless, his head held high.

"But I do not want you. As I mentioned earlier, I

have changed my mind and it's all because of your future mate here. Ever since I saw her last, I have had the taste of her in my mouth. It made me realize ... why have an Alpha under my control when I could sire the perfect weapon."

I felt his fangs graze against my pulse, his breath heating my already fevered skin. I moaned, breaking contact with Mason because I was too embarrassed by my reaction.

He saw my intentions and whispered my name. Looking back up, he mouthed the words to be strong and I nodded. He needed me to keep focused and not get lost in my head. I instantly stopped moaning, refusing to give Avery the satisfaction of hearing me.

"You mean to turn her? Is that your master plan?" Mason sounded unbelieving.

Fear quickly replaced whatever desire I was feeling. I didn't want to become a vampire. I loved being a werewolf, and I began to struggle against the vampire holding me. But it lasted a brief moment before the contact sent me straight back into pleasure and I writhed.

"Of course I am, only a fool would pass by the opportunity to tap into her power. She will be the weapon I use to crush Zane and take over, the people flocking to follow her cause after she reveals how her beloved mate was slaughtered by the vampire king."

"You're mad," he bellowed, tugging again on his restraints. "You greatly overestimate the influence I hold. Again, killing me will only fuel her anger, ensuring she'll never help you—sire or not. You may be able to compel her mind, but you will never govern her heart."

"Enough!" It was the only warning I had before

I felt razor sharp teeth pierce my skin, latching onto my neck, and the immediate draw of blood from my artery.

Avery's body hardened and I soon found myself lost in the erotic sensation of his feeding. I tried not to moan, but it only made me sound louder. I tried not to let my hands wander, but I found myself reaching behind for any part of him I could.

I felt myself growing weaker, and made one more attempt to break free, knowing it was my last chance, Remembering Daniel's instruction I slammed my head back, hitting Avery with such a force, it broke his connection with my neck, causing him to temporarily let me go.

Dropping to the floor, I let my wolf rip free, rushing to the forefront. Fur rippled over me as I rose on all fours. There was no joy in the change, no sense of wonder at the prospect of a run under the moon.

I snarled—my lips curling back from my teeth, and I felt my hackles rise. My ears flattened against my head, and a strand of saliva dripped from my jaw. I lunged forward, aiming for the vampire's jugular.

Using his supernatural reflexes, he dodged my attack, and with a disappointed tone, chastised me. "Come now, there's no need for this. Be a good doggy and change back."

I paced, looking for a weakness to take advantage of, all the while never giving him access to my mate. We tested each opening I found, but the vampire was strong and not easily fooled. Knowing time was of the essence, we faked a leap to the left, twisting at the last moment, and caught his shoulder in between my teeth. The bitter taste of his blood flooded my taste buds and I clamped down hard, shaking my head back and forth as chunks of flesh came away in my mouth.

This caused a reaction from my enemy, his fangs fully descending, and he flew at me, his hands curled into claw-like weapons.

I was ready though, springing off my hind legs, and we collided in midair. I could hear Mason yelling, trying to distract Avery.

Sharp fingernails gouged into my side, and I felt my blood begin to flow. I didn't focus on the pain though, and instead snapped harder with my own fangs, narrowly missing his throat.

He tried to wrap his arm around my center, but I twisted and turned again, wrestling him onto the floor where I finally got him pinned, and moved in for the kill.

I saw something move out of the corner of my eye, and noticed of Avery's minions had entered the room.

My focus shifted, and seizing the opportunity, Avery lunged forward. He latched back onto my throat, drinking in mouthfuls of blood, intent on continuing my transition.

I felt myself divide from my wolf, and could hear her howl from the looming weakness. We couldn't keep united, and I changed back.

I raised my hands up and tried to pry Avery off me. Lifting my knee, I attempted to connect with his body. I hit him and he paused for a moment. I drew in a steadying breath and commanded myself to stay awake. If I could distract him from feeding more, I'd be able to heal and replenish—not completely, but enough to keep fighting.

Worried about the new arrival, I glanced in his direction just in time to see him disintegrate before my eyes. Without warning, the weight holding my body down disappeared, and I suddenly showered with ashes. I screamed, finding myself free, and I scrambled to protect myself from the new threat.

But there was no threat.

Devlin, bloodied and barely able to keep himself standing, threw me a weary grin before he dropped to his knees, a makeshift stake clattering to the floor beside him. A quick glance over his body told me he was already starting to heal, but the blood loss was making it a slow process.

Tearing at my wrist, blood beginning to drip, I knelt beside my friend and protector to offer him freely what he needed. I begged him to drink but he stubbornly refused, muttering about blood oaths and honor. I tried holding the gash over his mouth, but he turned his head, still too weak to move and sit up.

I looked over at Mason, concerned. I had a vampire on the verge of passing out from blood loss, and a werewolf chained to the wall by silver. I couldn't help either, and I slumped back onto my bottom to think.

Mason's weary voice finally offered the solution. "Have him remove the chains, Darcy. They're vampire created so he can break the spell on the locks. Then drag him over here so I can feed him. With the silver no longer touching my skin, I'll heal quickly."

As I went to move, I heard Devlin begin to chant the needed words, and the manacles holding Mason popped open, allowing him to drop to the ground.

I rushed over to the weakened vampire, and dragged his heavy body over to where Mason lay.

Mason moved slowly, and I helped him with Devlin's dagger when he had difficulty ripping his skin. Placing his wrist over Devlin's open mouth, he leaned in and whispered his gratitude. The sharing of blood with supernatural being of extreme power was not usually done because it provided the receiver with a potent boost in abilities.

This wasn't a gift given lightly. I knew Mason felt bound to honor the one who had saved my life, and in turn saved his.

As we two watched Devlin, he lashed out suddenly and took a death grip on the offered wrist. I could see the giant gulps of blood he was taking. Mason lay down completely, and I worried the feeding was going too far.

With a swirl of his tongue, the now recovering vampire sealed the wounds and released Mason's arm. Both men lay side by side, and I pulled my knees in tight, waiting for them to become more aware. It was always fascinating to me, watching the healing process of others, and sooner than I expected, I saw Devlin slowly sit up and look around.

He must have noticed my lack of clothing, the change shredding what I'd been wearing, and he gave me his shirt. It was incredibly large, coming to just above my knees, but I was grateful to be covered again. After everything that had happened, I felt a little vulnerable.

"You doing okay? In one piece?" Devlin asked. He checked me over vigorously, turned me this way and that before he was satisfied. "Remind me when this is over I need to beat you for getting me into these situations."

"What did you expect? She's a magnet for trouble," Mason's voice came in a soft groan. His eyes were opened, and I rushed over to help him stand.

"What do you mean she's a magnet? I thought trouble was her middle name," a voice from the door joked, followed by a cough. We all looked over and found Daniel leaning against on one of the shelves, rubbing his head. "What the hell happened? One minute Mason was telling me we were leaving, and the next I woke up shoved in a closet."

"It's a long story, but before you all get started, can we do this at home?" I looked to the men, hopeful. I was rewarded with a resounding yes, and we slowly made our way back up the stairs.

Mason needed a little help at first, but as we got closer to the main floor, he took control. He was the Alpha, and despite his ordeal, he had an image of strength to protect.

I was amazed to find dead bodies as we exited the house. I'd assumed Avery's minions would all be vampires, but he'd managed to also recruit humans. Some of the Enforcers had begun the clean-up and removal process.

Mentioning to Mason he'd join us later for a debriefing, Devlin quickly gave me a hug and I thanked him before watching him climb on his bike and drive away. I had a lot of questions for him, and I wasn't going to rest until he answered them.

"You ready?" Mason's arms wrapped around my waist, and I rested my head on his shoulder.

I nodded, eager to put this behind us. I climbed into the SUV, and didn't look back.

By tomorrow this would all be in the past, and as I looked at Mason, anticipation for the future grew. Yeah, things could only get better from here.

Chapter Twenty

The flickering of the candlelight caused soft shadows to dance around the room. The night had been complete perfection, and as I watched Mason push his plate away with a look of satisfaction across his face, I deemed the dinner a success.

It'd taken a few days to get everything squared away, the business of Avery and his attempt to overthrow Zane finally put to rest. There had been countless meetings, the bouncing back and forth of ideas between leaders, precautions put into place with the hope of preventing something like this in the future.

Mason didn't hold out much hope, believing there would always be someone with more greed and pride than common sense. He believed in the alliance, and it was stronger than ever. The events hadn't turned him bitter, if anything he was more determined to protect his pack.

Smiling across the table, I couldn't help the sigh of relief I let out. I'd been able to smuggle him away from everything for a night of pampering like I'd wanted. At first, my plan had revolved around him, making sure he knew he was supported and loved, but as the night progressed, the focus rested on both of us. We were a couple—there wasn't one without the other.

"So, did you enjoy the dinner?" I glanced over at his empty plate. It seemed silly to ask because there were a few moments where I wondered if he'd pick up his dish and lick it clean. It was something he would do, especially when he was in a goofy mood.

"It was delicious, Darcy. I enjoyed every mouthful. In fact, you need to tell me your secret." There was a twinkle in his eye, and I blushed.

Please tell me he didn't figure it out, I thought. "What do you mean?" I spoke aloud, chewing on my bottom lip.

"Correct me if I'm wrong, but I swear this tasted just like the chicken fettuccine from Mama Alder's Kitchen. How'd you manage that?" Dipping his finger into the remaining sauce, he swirled it around his plate before licking it off his finger. "I can't get enough."

I could feel the heat on my face, and prayed the light from the candles would hide some of my embarrassment. There was no fooling this man, and I avoided looking him in eye.

"Well ... you see ...," I stuttered, trying to explain how I had no other choice than to quickly order out, the meal I planned was burnt to a crisp, and now lay hidden in the trash bin outside.

"It's okay, sweetheart. It doesn't matter where it came from—it's the thought that counts. You did an amazing job, so thank you." He took one last sip of his drink, emptying the glass before rising to his feet. Walking over to the counter, he turned up the soft music I had playing, and standing before me, extended his hand. "Would you dance with me?"

Tingles erupted over my skin, my heart beginning to race as I looked up into the face of the man I loved. He was breathtaking, his masculine beauty still causing an affect. "There's nowhere I'd rather be than in your arms."

The smile he offered melted my insides, and he pulled me up into his embrace as we slowly began to move back and forth to the sound of the melody. I loved the intimacy of the moment—the closeness, and how our bodies seemed to fit just right.

"Sorry about dinner. I worked so hard and wanted everything to be perfect." I rested my head against his shoulder, murmuring into his shirt. "One day, I'll be able to cook a meal to completion without Daniel needing to run in with a fire extinguisher."

Mason chuckled, and I felt him tighten his hold as he bent his head forward to whisper near my ear. "You're wrong, sweetheart. Tonight was perfect, but not because of dinner. You're the reason, and this is what makes it wonderful—being able to talk with you, touch you, and hold you close. You'll always be the best part of my day and why I look forward to the rest of our life together. With you by my side, I have it all."

I brought our bodies to a stop, a feeling of wonder filling me. "How do you do that? Speak the words in my heart so beautifully. I love you, Mason, and there's nothing more I want than to be with you. You're my forever too—my happily ever after." I stretched upward and placed a kiss on his lips.

"You know there is one thing that would make this night flawless, something that's been regrettably missing."

"Did I forget something?" I peered into his eyes, unsure if I understood what he meant.

"Dessert." He started at me hungrily, but the look was wasted.

"Oh, no. It's actually the one thing I didn't burn! Let me go get it so you can taste it." Without thinking, I began to pull away, and was promptly stopped by his hand tightening around my arm.

"I believe my dessert is right here, and you're right. I'm definitely going to taste and savor it."

Crushing his mouth down, his tongue swept past my lips and began to move slowly with mine, the gentleness of it becoming my undoing. My body felt like it was dissolving, as fire rushed through me, setting my insides aflame. I grabbed hold of him, using his strength to keep me from falling and I reveled in the feeling of security I found. He was mine and I was his— both the keepers of each other's hearts. I trusted him completely, and I submitted to his lead.

I felt my body being lifted, my feet leaving the floor, and instinctively I wrapped them around his hips. Where ever we touched, it left a trail of sensation, and with my arms around his neck, I tried to bring him even closer.

One hand was around my waist, securing me to him while the other was entwined in my hair. He tugged on it gently, causing my head to tilt backward, offering him better access. His tongue was relentless as his passion drove us deeper, the seal of our mouths never breaking as we shared a kiss worthy of the romance books I adored.

I heard the loud crash of dinnerware being swiped off onto the floor as Mason placed my bottom on the table. Pulling away, both of us breathing ragged, I laughed. "Was that really necessary?"

Lowering me backward, his body following, he stretched me out on the surface. "Of course, I was always told to eat at the table. I'm determined to show you my impeccable manners."

He didn't allow me to respond, bringing his mouth back to mine as he nibbled at my lips, tracing them with the tip of his tongue. Leaving trails of kisses across my cheek, he nestled into my neck and began to do the same there. I couldn't help but shiver as he sucked softly on me, finding the spot which always left me feeling addled.

"This is how you enjoy your sweets properly—savoring each bite—taking your time."

I couldn't speak, feeling completely ravished. All I could do was hold on tightly.

He worked his way back to my mouth, whispering as he did, "The mating ritual can't get here fast enough. I don't think I can wait that long. I want you, Darcy. I need you."

His words echoed in my mind and they ignited a storm of emotions inside. I wanted him just as bad, not just to help ease the burning that seemed to constantly be between us, but it was that final way of showing just how deeply I loved him.

Three more weeks, I kept telling myself, but the way I felt at this moment, it seemed like a lifetime away.

I'm not sure how, but I heard a knock.

Mason rested his forehead against mine, his hand stroking the side of my body, and he groaned. "Let someone else get it. I'm not finished with you."

"I sent everyone away tonight, remember? Besides, no finishing until we're finally mated." I sighed, finding it difficult to break away when all I wanted was to continue being lost in him. "We have a lifetime of this, so let's take a rain check and see who's at the door."

Reluctantly, he lifted me off the table, and helped me straighten my clothes. I laughed softly at the pained look on his face, stroking his arm as I brushed past him.

Whoever was there was getting impatient, judging from the steadily increasing pounds.

With Mason tagging behind, murmuring this

better be a matter of life or death, I swung the door open to find a woman in the process of leaving. She was almost down the steps, and the sound of my query caused her to turn.

"Can I help you?" I didn't recognize her, and wondered who she was here for.

"Mason?" A smile broke across her face, her eyes lighting up, and she pushed past me, throwing her arms around him.

My wolf raised her head, curious to see who this intruder was and we watched her pull his head down to hers, offering him an open mouth kiss. I couldn't keep quiet any longer.

"Who the hell are you?" I didn't bother keeping the anger out of my voice.

She turned around startled, as if surprised I was still standing there, but it was Mason who answered. He looked as shocked as I was, and I wanted to pull him away from her. He was mine, and she had no right to touch him the way she did.

"Darcy, this is ...," he couldn't finish the sentence.

The woman extended her hand, but I refused to shake it, folding my arms over my chest.

She drew herself in closer to the shell shocked Mason, wrapping her arms around his waist. "Amber. Mason's future mate." Her declaration crushed me, robbing my lungs of breath.

I stepped forward, looking her square in the eye. "Excuse me?" I said, and my wolf leapt to the surface.

About the Author

A homesick Aussie living amongst the cactus and mountains of Arizona, Belinda Boring is a self-proclaimed addict of romance and all things swoon worthy. When she's not devouring her latest read, you can find her celebrating her passion for books on her blog The Bookish Snob.

With all that excitement, it wasn't long before she began writing, pouring her imagination and creativity into the stories she dreams. Whether urban fantasy, paranormal romance or romance in general, Belinda strives to share great plots with heart and characters that you can't help but connect with. Of course, she wouldn't be Belinda without adding heroes she hopes will curl your toes.

Surrounded by a supportive cast of family, friends and the man she gives her heart and soul to, Belinda is living the good life. Happy reading!

Website: http://thebookishsnob.blogspot.com
Twitter: https://twitter.com/#!/thebookishsnob
Facebook: Bookish Snob

Coming Soon From

Moonstruck Media

BEST SELLING AUTHOR

CHASING
Nikki

LACEY WEATHERFORD

Chase Walker used to be a good kid—charming, athletic, and with a bright future ahead, but that was before travesty struck his life, sinking him into deep despair. Caught up in a world of drugs and alcohol, he doesn't notice time slipping away until he's arrested for underage drinking one night.

Fed up with watching her son destroy his life, Chase's mom relocates him to live in a small ranching community with his ex-military grandfather. Chase is far from happy about the situation until he meets, Nikki, the cute cheerleader who won't give football players like him the time of day.

Chase enjoys a good challenge though and sets out to claim Nikki for his own. He soon discovers she's more than a pretty face—she's a balm to his troubled spirit also. But when tragedy strikes Nikki's life too, suddenly the football season isn't just about winning, it's about chasing Nikki's dreams as well. Chase lays it all on the line to save the girl he loves.

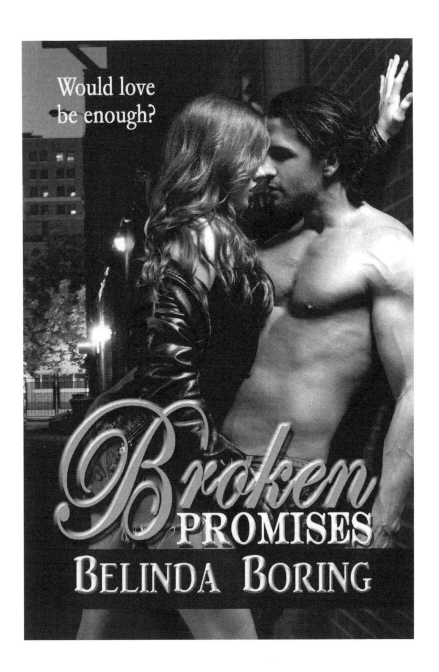

Would love
be enough?

Broken
PROMISES
BELINDA BORING

All Bree wanted to do was spend her Friday night with the man she loved and adored. Planning to watch a movie together, she never would've believed leaving her home would result in her relationship with Quinn being tested beyond its limits.

Unbeknownst to her, the Fae have been organizing to invade Earth, and their devious plans are culminating now, colliding with Bree's very existence. Using a powerful glamour, the Fae trigger each person's violent tendencies, turning the streets into a battleground and strangers against each other.

In a crushing blow, Quinn becomes affected and Bree finds herself battling to save her lover from himself as he stalks her relentlessly, taunting her at every turn. In a game of cat and mouse, Quinn can't decide whether he wants to seduce her or kill her, breaking her heart further with each encounter.

But fighting for her love isn't her only worry. As the battle ensues, Bree discovers a startling truth about her own heritage that she must come to terms with. Determined to bring balance back, she teams up with others to drive the Fae back across the veil, only to find herself in way over her head. Bree has no other choice but to fight, leading her to a confrontation that will change her world forever - and threaten to leave her with broken promises.

Sneak Peek

Broken Promises

Book One in the Brianna Lane series.

Prologue

In the private chambers of a world long kept hidden

"Enter."

The voice calling out through the door had a musical lilt to it—like the sound of tinkling bells moving against a gentle breeze, carrying it across the room within. To the unassuming listener, the image of innocence and childlike quality reflected in the sound, but to those who knew better, a coldness and indifference echoed just as loudly.

The Queen's advisor stood motionless, hand poised on the elegant handles leading to the Queen's private chambers. Even though he was new to the prestigious position and the one who was assigned the duty of reporting to the Queen, he still hesitated at the sound of her voice.

Images skated across his mind as memories of the last fool who had delivered less than pleasing news caused him to shudder. No one could ever guarantee the mood they would find her in—her reputation for fickleness well known throughout the court. Where some offered the excuse it was age that made her this way, truth was no one understood why. Everyone merely strived to find ways to survive her temper.

The advisor hoped she was in good spirits, but if not, would gladly settle for the bored and dismissive attitude she'd recently shown. However—knowing what he was about to share with her—there was a good chance she would unleash her fiery temper, and he would find himself joining his predecessor.

His hand trembled slightly as he continued to grip the entrance handle. It pained him to be this shaken because he was naturally strong in character, but he would be a fool not to recognize the danger he was stepping into.

"Unless you wish to find yourself in my dungeons, Orville, I would come through those doors now. I won't be kept waiting."

She knew it was him. He marveled a sound so beautiful to the ears could be equally as threatening and bracing himself, he swung the doors open, and stepped into the dimly lit room.

The first thing he noticed was the Queen wasn't in her usual spot and was currently sitting on the chaise by the brick hearth.

Part of her face was hidden in shadow, the other half flickering from the pale light given off by the fire she had blazing. Orville found his breath hitching as her undeniable beauty struck him.

His people were naturally a graceful, beautiful race which minstrels and poets had written about for countless ages. With just one glance, even the most uncreative and lacking in imagination were waxing poetic and as he approached his Ruler, Orville could see why.

Recently she had taken to having her hair weaved into intricate designs, feathering in the delicate flowers found only in his world. The blonde, almost white strands shimmered as the light reflected off them, causing her to seem as though her head was surrounded by a glowing aura.

Her face was that of perfection. Large, doe like eyes stood out, framed with the longest of lashes he had ever seen, giving her a very childlike, innocent appearance. Her pale blue eyes shimmered against her ivory skin and looked soft enough to touch.

Without a doubt, the Queen gave the image of everything innocent and pure, but he knew how deceptive those looks could be. Many a person had underestimated the Queen, believing her easily manipulated to their designs. Those buffoons were either still residing in the depths of her dungeons, or their heads were cruelly shoved on spikes—gruesomely displayed on the palace walls.

No, it was vital, if not crucial, to always remember the viciousness which lay deep within the heart of the Queen, and never be fooled.

Initially, he hoped the room would have been lighter so to see her expression—a quick way to judge how she would receive him. Without it, he needed to rely on the second thing he noticed since entering the room. Despite the gown she was wearing, and the many layers of soft taffeta and brocade, he could see her foot furiously tapping against the floor.

It was just as he feared. Something had obviously upset her, and he would be lucky to leave with his head intact.

With no other way of removing himself from the potential danger of her temper, he threw himself into a deep bow, holding it until she gave the words to release him.

"Your Majesty, excuse the interruption but it is important that I speak with you." He risked a brief peek through his fallen hair and saw she was looking at him with vague annoyance. Clearly he should have waited for a better time to deliver his message, but with the way things were unfolding, if he waited even a moment longer, it could spell certain disaster.

"I trust you are aware I have little patience this evening, Orville. So whatever it is you have to say, do so quickly, and then leave by the way you came in."

Her tone was abrupt, and if she had allowed him to lift himself from his bow, he would have seen the flash of anger in her eyes. With no other option but to remain staring at the carpet, Orville swallowed his pride and gathered himself before continuing.

"News has reached the court of a disturbance amongst the nobility. Someone has been secretly moving amongst the people and amassing a threat large enough to generate talk. The court gossip speculates a move is being made to cross over and if something isn't done to prevent it, it could mean misfortune for us all. The rumors are going as far to say if you don't take care of it, the citizens will overthrow you and place someone else on the throne." Orville held his breath and closed his eyes, waiting silently as the Queen digested what he had shared.

"And what do you think Orville? What do you speculate?" There was a veiled threat in the whisper that reached his ears. They had come quickly to the point in the conversation where he needed to tread carefully, his life hanging fragilely in the balance.

"I think, Your Majesty, it would be wise to investigate. I already have men waiting for my word to go into the city and learn all they can. I just wait for your approval."

He had barely finished talking before he realized she had moved, quietly crossing the distance between them. A wave of cold fear spread across him as he felt her bend down over and whisper softly in his ear.

"I don't care what you think. I don't care what the people think. I am Queen and my word is Law. Why should I be concerned what one person does? Tell me Orville, why should I care who crosses over?"

She placed her hand abruptly on the back of his head, forcing him into a bow so deep his nose threatened to touch his knees and land him face first onto the floor. Orville clenched his fists, struggling to hold his tongue.

It would do him no good to speak, to try and reason with her. She was clearly not interested in the threat, believing whatever was happening in her kingdom didn't affect her—especially with her hidden away in the safety of her palace.

"Don't annoy me with this gossip again or you will force me to show you my temper and cruelty. If this reaches my ears again, I will hold you personally responsible, and there won't be a rock you can hide under to escape my fury. Do you understand Orville?"

To push across her point, the Queen swept her leg forward to kick his feet out from under him, sending him sprawling across the floor.

Never in his life had he been treated this way—he'd never been made to suffer such indignity. Had anyone else treated him this way, he would have killed them where they stood—no questions asked.

Blood coursed through his veins, causing it to pound in his ears, adrenaline pumping through his system. Fighting against the urge to move, he lay there quietly. He killed any sign of defiance, in both his eyes and body language, knowing that even the slightest glimpse would end him.

"Yes, I think you understand. Now get up of floor and out of my sight."

The welcomed dismissal echoed through the room, and before the Queen could even turn to sit on her chair, Orville was up from the ground. A moment later, he was through the door and without another look, he fled.

In the quiet home of a world where staying hidden means survival

"The signs are all there, Ruth. Something is happening, and it has us worried. It has the animals scared, and poor Sally has retreated into her room, refusing to come out. We've tried looking through our ancient tomes for clues, but so far all we've been able to learn is that whatever's happening is going to be bad."

The voice on the other side of the phone sounded tired, and Ruth could only imagine the long hours that had gone into looking for answers before this call was made.

As the Highest Seer of their order, Ruth knew this call hadn't been an easy one for Michelle to make. She too had been feeling the mysterious murmurings and slight unease for the last few days and had started the process of sending out inquiries.

It turned out unnecessary as phone calls from around the world began pouring in—this being one of many she had taken tonight already.

Ruth ran her hand over her face, taking the brief moment to gather her thoughts and find the needed strength to stay awake. She hadn't slept for days, each time she closed her eyes, portents of alarm filling her mind.

Dragged from visions of great destruction, she'd sat up from a dead sleep, wrapped in her twisted bed sheets. Dripping in a cold sweat, her mind frantically tried to make sense of what she'd seen before the grip of sleep left her, and she was left with nothing but a few snippets of images. She would try to force herself back with the hope of learning more, but each time she'd awakened with nothing. The nightmares came when they chose to, and Ruth wasn't used to being so blind.

As the Highest Seer, hers were the powers to find insight through her dreams, but whatever was happening, it had found a way to block her ability and that alone left her shaken.

"The sisters are scared, Ruth. They look to me for answers, and I have nothing for them. They're starting to murmur amongst themselves, and I worry if we can't tell them something, they will go out looking themselves. If it's as bad as I feel it is, they'll only get themselves hurt, even killed."

"Have you gone out to the sacred grove there?" Ruth asked, closing her eyes. She held her breath for the response she knew was coming, her stomach clenched tightly with fear.

The groves were the cornerstone of all they held dear, places of infinite power. What may look like an ordinary cluster of trees and greenery to some were in fact magical hot spots, places where the veil between worlds were thin.

It was here visitors and intruders from other dimensions entered, and it was the sacred duty of those in her order to stand sentinel, guarding the world from those who would come to do it harm.

"Yes," Michelle whispered, the fear clearly in her voice as it began to tremble. "I made the trip this morning and what I felt there broke my heart. There's a darkness that feels like it's oozing out of the circle. I've never felt anything like it before, and I pray I never will. It doesn't look good Ruth. It doesn't look good at all."

There was silence as both women paused, waiting for the other one to be the first to say it. Ruth knew exactly what Michelle had felt—the same disturbing feeling had come over her when she'd gone to the nearby sacred grove this morning for answers. Something was definitely wrong. The thrum of power which usually coursed through her body and gave her clarity had left her nauseous and weak for the rest of the day. Something was altering the power, distorting it, and it all lead to the same conclusion. Michelle's report simply confirmed it.

"They're coming, aren't they?" the voice on the other end spoke softly. A lump rose in Ruth's throat as if to stop her from answering the question.

Every part of her screamed to deny the truth, that the occurrences were simply mad imaginings of an idle mind. Even as she opened her mouth to reply, Ruth choked on the words, a cold wave of dread sinking into her heart.

"Yes." It was all she could answer before hearing the shocked gasp from Michelle, and Ruth released her own breath of resignation. "There is only one reason for this change to be happening, and it doesn't bode well for us. The last time they came it almost destroyed the world."

"Is there anything we can do? Do you think there is anything in the writings which could help us?" Ruth could hear the plea in Michelle's voice—the need for a positive answer.

"I don't know. I would hope so. We have known of their existence for what seems like an age, and yet we're still here." The authority rang through her voice as she spoke with the power of her office. "Take aside a few sisters who you can trust and give them the assignment of searching. Tell them to talk with no one but you, and keep me informed."

"Yes, my Lady." Michelle formally replied, her voice stronger, lined with a new found sense of determination. "I know just who to ask, and hopefully by the end of today we'll have learned something helpful."

As the conversation came to a close, a feeling crashed over Ruth she knew couldn't be ignored and before she wished Michelle luck and Godspeed, she added. "And Michelle, as gently as you can, let your sisters know it might be best to talk with their families ... to at least warn them. If it gets as bad as I think it will, things could move quickly, and there may not be much time later. Remind them the importance of not causing panic to spread, and do what you can to ease their fears. It's only as a precaution, but the Spirit whispers to me it's necessary."

"I'll see to it straight away." Michelle replied, as she made plans to check in later and hung up.

Ruth stood for a moment with the receiver in her hand, hearing the empty dial tone beeping. It was done and the order given. Michelle had been the last of the sisters to call. They were all aware now, and the only thing left to do was prepare—wait and pray they'd be ready for the threat coming.

Ruth sighed and braced herself for what she needed to do next. With great reluctance, knowing she was about to change the world of the one she cherished most—she lifted the receiver back to her ear and began dialing.

Please let me say the right words, she chanted, as she waited for the other end to pick up. *And please, forgive me for the promise I'm about to break.*

Made in the USA
San Bernardino, CA
04 November 2012